Stolen Magic at the Onami Fair

A Keveren Auberel Mystery

Nikki Bollman

STICKS & SCRIBBLES PRESS

First paperback edition July 2023

Cover background image by RDNichols on shutterstock.com

Cover image of book by AVA Bitter on shutterstock.com

Cover image of rats by KOV777 on shutterstock.com

Cover design by Nikki Bollman

ISBN 979-8-9863942-2-0 (paperback)

ISBN 979-8-9863942-3-7 (hardcover)

Published by Sticks & Scribbles Press

www.sticksandscribbles.com

 Created with Vellum

CRAFTMAGIC

Keveren Auberel sat at a table in an alcove in a back corner of her favorite library at the Scholar's Tower. She flipped through her book—about paper magic—to a page with a detailed explanation of how a mage could write with ink on paper without using a pen or their hands in any way, then groaned and flipped the book shut. She buried her face in her hands and sank to the table.

She had been trying for weeks to discover any information at all about her recently discovered power, sketchmagic, as she liked to call it to herself, but her search had been fruitless. Although she had a book from her former teacher about craftmagic, she had read every page in it front to back several times over the summer, and now she wanted to know more. Yet her searches in the Scholar's Tower's many libraries had proven fruitless.

The Tower had several libraries scattered throughout its hodgepodge of buildings, but this one was the oldest, and, Kev thought, the most interesting. Its sturdy but aging wooden shelves held books upon books about magic of all different kinds, spanning back centuries. The building had three floors, and each floor had many nooks, crannies, and alcoves with seats, tables, and windowsills to sit on or study at. It was perfect for finding a quiet place to study, whether it be for her classes or her own ends.

"There you are!"

Kev looked up from her book. It was her friend Ferra, who was a year ahead of her at the Scholar's Tower.

Kev closed her book and pulled her notes and journal over it as Ferra approached her table.

There was another girl with Ferra, too. She trailed behind Ferra, a hesitant smile on her lips that looked like it might skitter away at any moment. Kev thought the girl's eyes might be watering a little, too, so she tried to give an encouraging smile despite her foul mood.

"You were looking for me?" Kev asked Ferra as she slid into a chair across the table from Kev. The other girl took the chair next to Ferra.

Ferra placed both hands on the table, palms flat, and leaned toward Kev with a grin.

"We need your help."

Something about the look in Ferra's eyes told Kev that the help didn't involve studying.

"Oh?" was all Kev managed to say in response.

"This is Lyria," Ferra said, gesturing at her companion. "She needs our help finding something."

"What kind of help?" Kev asked slowly, though she suspected she knew what Ferra was getting at. Ferra knew about Kev's sketches and the role they'd played in tracking down a small magical dragon, called a weyrdragon, last spring. In fact, Kev's attempts to find the weyrdragon were how she'd met Ferra in the first place, as well as their friend Eldet, who was the son of one of the dragon riders at the dragon rider outpost in Mirella.

"It's okay if you don't want to," Lyria said in a rush, then turned to Ferra. "Really, I can find more supplies at the market, and my ma can get me new tools."

"But then you won't be able to sell anything at the fair," said

Ferra. She put her hand on Lyria's arm. "It's okay, Kev will help us."

Ferra turned to Kev with a beaming smile.

"The fair?" Kev said, interested now.

Lyria blushed. "Oh, yes. Well, I'm Onami, so my family sells at the fair every year, obviously, but after that I stay in Mirella for the year, since I'm studying here." She gestured around herself to indicate the Scholar's Tower.

"What do you sell?" Kev asked. "My ma trades at the fair every year. She sells wool and dyestuffs."

"Oh, I sell jewelry and hair decorations that I make." Lyria's face lit up as she began to talk about her craft. She wore some of her jewelry on her wrists and about her neck, which she showed to Kev. It was made with an assortment of colored beads in all materials, woven together with knotted cord in various designs.

"So that's what you lost?" Kev asked as she admired a bracelet that Lyria had given her to look at.

"My whole jewelry case, with all of my supplies and tools, as well as more than half of the pieces I had made for the fair this year," said Lyria. "It was supposed to have a protection on it," she added. She opened her mouth as if to say something more, but then stopped and drummed her fingers on the table.

"And the fair isn't here much longer," Kev commented.

Lyria nodded. "Two and a half more weeks."

"Tell her about the other thing," Ferra said.

"Oh, it's probably nothing," said Lyria. "I was probably imagining it. I think."

Ferra pursed her lips and stared pointedly at Lyria.

"Fine, fine," said Lyria, then looked to Kev again. "My case disappeared when I was at the Flowermiller Cafe. That's the one near here, in Crafter's Square. I was sitting at a table inside and working one of my bracelets. The case was by my feet because I had all that I needed for the bracelets on the table in front of me. But then when I picked up one of the beads, it felt hot, like it burned, but there was a little more to the feeling, too. It was so strange. It surprised me so much that I yelped and dropped it. It rolled away, so I got up to get it. When I sat back down, my case was missing. And the bead wasn't hot anymore."

"What kind of bead was it?" Kev asked. "Was there a mage around? Do you still have the bead?" Kev couldn't help it; she was intrigued by Lyria's story.

"I don't know about any mages," said Lyria. "It's just a normal cafe, so there could have been mages, but not any obvious ones."

She reached into the satchel that rested on her lap and pulled out another bracelet like the ones she wore.

"It was this one," she said, and pointed to a smooth, gray bead woven into the pattern of the red cord. She handed the bracelet to Kev.

Kev touched the bead. It looked like the stones that lined the beaches around the shores of Lake Morna.

"Lake stone?" she asked.

Lyria nodded.

Kev rubbed her thumb up and down the surface of the bead. It was flat and almost perfectly round, like a disc whose edges had been worn smooth. The hole was drilled through the flat part of the bead, so that the disc lay flat on her palm.

"You could paint or engrave on the face of it," Kev murmured.

"I do, sometimes," Lyria said. "You're right, this one is perfect for it." Her face lit up as she spoke, but then fell. "Except my engraving tools were in my case."

"So you see why we need your help," Ferra said eagerly. "If you could maybe come to the cafe with us, maybe draw a little, and draw the bracelet too, maybe there would be something that would tell us what happened to the case!"

While Ferra pleaded, Kev stared at the bracelet in her palm. Lyria was truly a gifted craftsperson, Kev could tell.

"Can I keep this for a bit?" Kev asked, holding up the bracelet. "To help me draw it?"

"Of course," said Lyria. "Anything that will help."

"So you'll come to the cafe with us?" Ferra asked. "We're going tomorrow."

"I'll come," Kev said. "But I can't promise anything. I don't really even know if my drawing works like that." She had done little tests to see if she could use her drawings for scrying, like she'd done with the weyrdragon, but she hadn't yet successfully reproduced the effect.

A distant bell sounded, letting them know that the next class period would begin in ten minutes. Kev gave one last glance at the book on paper magic and closed it. It wasn't going to be any use to her. She took the bracelet from the table, then opened her satchel. Looking into her satchel, she barely stifled a squeak of surprise. Then she groaned.

"How did you get in there?" she said to the furry faces staring up at her from inside her satchel.

Since school had started, Kev had been unable to keep her two pet rats, Green Bean and Turnip, from following her to school each day. She left them in their cage each morning when she left for her classes, but since the rats had been mage raised, they were unusually smart, and had several seemingly magic talents. One of those talents was the ability to get themselves out of any enclosed space. Like their cage.

The rats also seemed to be inordinately good at following Kev without her knowing, and also avoiding being seen by anyone else. Though they often showed up in her satchel at the Scholar's Tower, Kev didn't think anyone else had ever seen them. She shrugged to herself. They were rats, after all. Even if they didn't have some kind of magic, they would probably still be fairly good at passing through streets and halls unnoticed.

"They found you again?" Ferra asked. She held out a hand to the opening of Kev's satchel, and Turnip immediately climbed into it. Ferra snuggled Turnip close to her and found a small treat in her pocket to give to the rat. Turnip nibbled it happily from her perch on Ferra's arm and seemed to stare at

Kev with a satisfied expression. Ferra handed Green Bean a treat of her own.

"Don't encourage them," Kev said.

"Who are they?" asked Lyria, leaning toward Ferra with a smile.

"Just my stubborn, ill-behaved pet rats," Kev said with a sigh. "I tried to get them to stay home."

"They're actually very well behaved, if you think about it," Ferra said. "Even though they follow you to school every day, nobody has ever seen them, and they've never caused any trouble." She held Turnip out toward Lyria. "Want to hold her? She really likes scratches behind her ears."

Lyria laughed and accepted the proffered rat. She let out a gasp when Turnip hopped up her arm, onto her shoulder, and burrowed under her hair.

"That tickles!"

"I'm sorry," Kev said, and started to reach out to take Turnip back.

"It's okay. She's soft!" Lyria leaned her head to the side so that her cheek brushed against Turnip's side.

"Oh, well that's not the reaction the rats usually get," Kev said with a wobbly laugh.

"Lyria likes animals a lot," Ferra said. "Probably about as much as Eldet."

Another bell chimed, reminding the girls that their next class would be starting soon.

"I guess I should give her back," Lyria said, and gently plucked Turnip from her shoulder and comfortably cradled her in both hands as she handed her back to Kev.

Ferra was right, Lyria was comfortable with animals, judging from the gentle way she handled Turnip and seemed to know how to support her properly.

Turnip happily slid back into the satchel with Green Bean, and Kev shook her head at the rats as she closed the flap over them once more.

"They've been good about keeping hidden so far," Kev said. "Let's just hope they can keep it up."

The three girls left the secluded library alcove and made their way out into the larger airy halls of the school. Kev parted ways with Ferra and Lyria and walked on to her next class with her hand securely on the flap of her satchel. Once again, she'd left the library with more questions than answers. How could she learn more about her craftmagic, what had happened to Lyria's satchel, and how in the world was Kev going to convince her rats that they could not come to school with her?

HISTORY OF MAGIC

Kev's next class, History of Magic, was taught by Mage Carrick Valaso. Mostly, students at the Scholar's Tower didn't study magic; they weren't mages. The mage academy was where the mage students went to learn their craft. But the Scholar's Tower was of the opinion that all students in Arethia should have a thorough understanding of magic and how it came to be used as it was in Arethia. Thus, History of Magic was one of the classes that all students at the Scholar's Tower took in their first year.

Kev slid into her seat just as the clock chimed the start of the hour. Cautiously, she lifted the flap of her satchel, bracing herself for an explosion of whiskered noses. But, true to their talent for remaining unseen, the rats cuddled at the bottom of her satchel alongside her books. Since she would draw her classmates' attention by whispering into her satchel, Kev held back the urge to hiss a warning to the rats to stay inside. Instead, she just stared at them and thought the warnings really hard in their direction before plucking her class notebook from the satchel.

When she turned forward at her table, she found herself staring into the haughty expression of Tanar, a tall boy with short black hair and intense dark eyes to match. He stared at Kev without saying anything.

"What?" Kev whispered.

Tanar's eyes flicked down toward her satchel, then he met Kev's eyes again, then turned around without a word.

What was that all about? Kev thought, though her stomach began to churn. Tanar was the last person she needed to notice her rats at school. But if he had, why hadn't he said anything? In these first few weeks of school, she'd learned that he was not the type of person to be afraid to voice any thought or concern that graced his mind. She'd also learned that he had taken a dislike to her, for reasons she could not fathom.

Mage Valaso strode briskly into the room and settled a pile of books on the podium before him. He was a tall and lanky man with light brown hair past his ears that seemed perpetually mussed. His tunic was blue with silver embroidery around the edges in a pattern of celestial shapes, mimicking a mage's full robe setup, but much more practical outside the halls of the Mage Academy. He perched on the stool in front of the podium, flipped open one of his large tomes, and cleared his throat.

Tanar leaned back in his chair, arms crossed, head tilted slightly to the side, as if he were entertaining the argument of another student set against him in a debate, not as if he were listening to the words of a renowned mage. Kev knew she shouldn't let Tanar's attitude bother her, but it did. Who was he to act so dismissive to their teacher, and to Mage Carrick Valaso at that, one of Mirella's most well-known mages?

Kev did her best to ignore Tanar and listen to Mage Valaso and take notes on his lecture.

Although Kev found the class interesting, she did sometimes wonder if it was really necessary. Everyone knew about magic; mages were all around them in Arethia. They ranged from the mage guard, who patrolled the streets and caught thieves or broke up fights, to carters and dockworkers like the ones her da worked with in the dockyards, to those who studied and researched at the Mage Academy beyond the normal training that every mage got.

Mage Valaso was talking about free magic, which was what Arethians practiced, and its counterpart bound magic, which was forbidden in Arethia, but used elsewhere in the world. Free magic meant that the mage used the magic in the environment around them and channeled it through their own talents and abilities to make things happen. They could use a special sight called mage sight to see the types of magic and then they could use their power to harness it. The only way that free magic could be used was for a mage to be present and to do the spell themselves, that way the mage would always be fully in control of their working and could adapt it to whatever circumstance they were in.

Bound magic meant that a mage took the energies they harnessed and, instead of using them right then, they trapped the energy into an object of some kind for later. This was dangerous, because an object could be made to hold too much magic and could behave unpredictably, and moreover, the magic might be activated by someone who was not a mage. Then the spell could not be controlled by anyone, and the consequences would be grim.

Kev frowned as she took down her notes on Mage Valaso's lecture. He recounted tales of bound magic gone awry in far distant Arethian history: a cookfire spell that burned down an entire village, a wind spell that turned into a great storm on Lake Morna and sank dozens of ships, and a defense spell that killed its owner rather than protecting them. She was familiar with these types of tales; she remembered hearing so many like them as she grew up. Magic was not for everybody, the tales said, and there was danger in putting it in talismans and charms and letting anyone use it. Therefore, bound magic was forbidden in Arethia.

But was there something in between bound magic and free magic? Or something that was just different? Kev's discovery of her sketchmagic talent made her wonder. She was definitely not a mage, yet she could draw pictures that showed the future—or at least a little bit of the present.

"Of course, there are some types of magic that are harder to place into one category or the other," Mage Valaso said, and Kev looked up from her notes.

"Say, for example, a mage who uses their talent while sowing seeds in a garden. If the seeds, and then the plants, take on some benefit from that magic that persists past the mage's own workings on it, is that free magic or bound magic?" He looked around the room and waited, showing that he was expecting an answer.

"You mean the plant is magic?" It was Tanar, and he said it in a scoffing voice. "Bound magic. Forbidden. Mages can only wield magic that they mean to use themselves at the time of the spell. If they leave it behind in their working, they are violating the ban on bound magic."

"Fair point," said Mage Valaso, inclining his head in Tanar's direction. "But is the plant really storing the magic that the mage used?"

"The plant didn't exist when the mage used their magic, only the seeds," Kev said. "So any magic in the plant wasn't really put there by the mage, exactly."

Mage Valaso gestured toward Kev. "Yes, very good. So while it's clear that if a mage takes magical energy and pours it into a stone or gem with the purpose of storing it, there are other times where the distinction is not so clear. It is a subject of much debate among mage scholars."

As Mage Valaso carried on with his lecture, Tanar glanced back at Kev with a smirk and rolled his eyes before turning forward again. Kev shook her head to herself and continued taking notes.

Mage Valaso was saying that the line between bound and free magic wasn't as clear as she'd always thought. Although, until Mage Maren had given her the craftmagic book, Kev hadn't really thought that much about it at all. Like all Arethians, she just knew that free magic was good, and bound magic was bad. The mage guard would take anyone caught using bound magic. Even merchants from beyond Arethia's borders knew that their mages had to refrain from using their magic when they were in port or in the markets.

When the lecture ended, Kev slowly opened her satchel before packing away her books so she could make sure that the rats weren't going to show their faces. They were still sleeping at the bottom of the bag, and Kev carefully placed her notebook back in to the satchel without disturbing them.

The bells chimed the end of the hour, and the students spilled out into the hallway. Kev was headed home now; she had no more classes for the day. She found herself walking behind Tanar and his friend Yeran from class. The two boys were laughing.

"I don't think we'll learn much about magic from this mage anyway," Tanar said. "Scholar mages are just failed practical mages. This class is just for those students who come from their tiny farm towns and know nothing about real magic. My ma said I shouldn't have to take it, but the Tower wouldn't allow it. It's required." His voice dripped disdain on the last word.

Yeran laughed. "My da said the same, why should I have to learn it when we have our household mages around all the time? Besides, bound magic isn't even real. Free magic is the only true magic."

Kev fought the urge to break into the boys' conversation. Not real? Who were they to say that a whole type of magic wasn't real? After they'd just had a lecture from a mage himself about the topic. But Tanar had just derided Mage Valaso as a scholar mage. And household mages? Tanar and his friend must be from merchant households, maybe a lesser noble house. She shook her head to clear her thoughts of them. It didn't matter. She would try to sit somewhere else next class so she didn't have to observe Tanar's nonverbal commentary on Mage Valaso's lectures.

Once outside, she tucked her hand into her satchel to pet the rats, only to find that they weren't there. Only books and her pen case met her fingertips. She glanced around the grassy yard and paths outside the Scholar's Tower, but she knew she wouldn't see them. They never let themselves be seen.

"How do they do that?" she wondered. "And where did they go?"

IN MA'S GARDEN

Kev didn't see Turnip and Green Bean again until she arrived home and passed through the house to her mother's garden in back. She found her mother at her work table by the back door, with Green Bean sitting on the table beside her, eating something, and Turnip perched on Ma's shoulder, face peeking out from under her hair.

"Oh there you are," Kev said with a laugh.

"Where did you expect to find me?" Ma said.

"Not you, the rats. They turned up in my bag at the Scholar's Tower again." She scooped her hand under Green Bean and brought her to her own shoulder. "I don't even know how they got here so fast."

"They certainly have some talents, don't they?"

"I just wish I knew what they all were," Kev replied. "So, what can I help with?"

Kev's mother was deep in the midst of preparing for the Onami fair and market. She grew dye plants in her garden behind the house and used them to color yarn and thread, which she sold to people throughout Mirella. In the fall, when the Onami caravans came to the outskirts of town and stayed for several weeks, was her mother's chance to sell or barter many of her yarns to the Onami in exchange for fleece, undyed yarn, and dried plants and seeds that could not be found in or near Mirella.

The garden behind their house glowed golden in the autumn afternoon sun. Against the back side of the house, baskets and bags full with yarn were piled on her ma's sturdy work tables. Farther away from the house, on a brick patio, dye pots simmered over a glowing woodstove.

Ma went into the shed and emerged with another basket brimming with yarn in her arms.

"Could you help me sort these out?" her mother asked. "By color, I think," she said, setting the basket on the workbench. "Yes, by color."

"I've got it, Ma," Kev said.

Her ma beamed. "I've got more after that," she said. Then her face fell. "Much more. Oh..." She pursed her lips and glanced back at the shed.

"The caravan's here for three more weeks," Kev said. "We'll have plenty of time to bring it all."

Her mother sighed. "You're right, of course. It's just so much to think about, this time of year," she said. "Oh, I'd better check those," she said, and bustled over to her dye pots.

Kev set about taking the skeins of yarn from the basket and arranging them into piles on the workbench by color. Once that was sorted, she fetched netted market bags from the shed, made with linen in an open net-like pattern so the yarn could be seen without opening the bag. When the bags were full, she hung them by their handles on hooks on the back wall of the house above the workbench. A roof protected the space behind the house over the workbench area in case of rain, so they could leave all of the yarn until the morning, when they would go to the Onami market early.

The yarn sorted and the dye pots tended to, Kev's ma brought out clay jars from the shed next. Kev knew what to do with these. Each jar held a different type of dried dye plant. The smaller jars held seeds that her mother had saved. Kev and her mother stood together at the workbench with the jars and folded paper bags, making up packets of dye plants and seeds. The Onami might use some of these themselves, but they would also carry them south on their caravan route and sell or trade them at other towns and in the city of Areth.

"What does it mean if someone says there was a protection on something, like a bag?" Kev said as they worked. Her mind had wandered to Lyria and her jewelry case at the sight of some seeds that reminded her of some of Lyria's beads.

"Who said that?" Kev's ma asked.

"Ferra's friend, Lyria. She stays in Mirella to go to the Scholar's Tower, but she's Onami." Kev explained what had happened with Lyria's project case. "She said it had a protection on it, but then she got quiet after that."

"Mm, I see."

Green Bean had climbed down from Kev's shoulder and now wandered along the back of the work table. She stood on her hind legs to sniff the top of the jar that Kev was scooping seeds from. Kev petted the rat's head with a finger.

"It made me think of magic, but tying magic to something to protect it, without the mage there, that would be bound magic, wouldn't it?" Kev asked.

"If only it were so simple," Kev's mother said with a rueful grin. "Magic works in different ways for different people, but the laws don't really take that into account. Mages don't take it into account, most of them."

"How is it not simple? I thought they just couldn't put magic into objects. A mage has to control the magic, so he can't put magic into things that will work away from him. Or her."

"Yes, they can't store magic in an object and accumulate power beyond their ability to control, or that someone without their skill in magic could use and be a danger. But, take your rats, for instance." Her ma reached her hand out to Green Bean, who happily climbed into it. Ma held the rat close to her and stroked her back as she spoke.

"A mage raised them, and who knows what he did, but they are different than normal pet rats. Smarter, and with some abilities with magic. Does that mean the mage put magic into them? Are the rats themselves bound magic?"

Kev's nose wrinkled as she thought of this. Just like Mage Valaso's plants in his example in class that day. Live things couldn't be bound magic. Bound magic meant storing magic in a gemstone, or making a lamp that would burn all on its own, without a mage there to keep it going. That was what could get mages into trouble, because bound magic was dangerous and unpredictable, and regular people without magic could get hurt, or worse. But the rats were just themselves.

Kev told her ma about Mage Valaso's lecture in class that day, including Tanar and Yeran's derisive comments afterward.

"Hm, yes, some people see it that way. But I know it's not so simple. So your friend's project bag. Did a mage pour magic into it to store and bind to it? I can't say. But what if the maker of the cloth had a little magic that helped them weave it? And then the person who sewed it all together was the same. Some Onami believe that a maker puts a little bit of magic into everything she makes. To them, it's not like bound magic. But mages...they don't always see the difference."

"Do you believe that? About making?"

Her ma smiled as she plucked a pinch of dried woad seeds from her jar and dropped them into a bag. "We're Senemi," she said. "We made a choice to abide by the rules of the city when we left the caravan to settle here." She dabbed a bit of glue on the side of the bag and folded the top of it down so it sealed. "We need to be careful."

Kev frowned. She watched her mother's hands pinch the long papery woad seeds and drop them into the next little paper envelope. They made a little scratching sound on the side of the paper as her mom shook the bag to settle them at the bottom.

She wanted to ask, now, did her mother use magic in her garden? Her dye baths? Her spinning? But it seemed wrong right now, like it would be improper, somehow. She sighed and kept packing seeds.

They continued to work until the sky started to shift toward twilight, then went in to prepare supper. After supper, Kev went up to her room to do her readings for the night.

But her mind wandered as she read, and she finally gave up and took out her sketchbook. As she drew, thoughts of craft-magic, bound magic, and free magic, and her mother's words about being careful as a Senemi filled her mind. She knew that some Arethians thought Senemi to be a little odd, and that they had similar feelings about the Onami. Some even refused to go to the fair or acknowledge the caravans' passing when Onami traveled through Mirella. But Kev had always thought that it was just a small group of stubborn people, stuck in their ways.

She herself had never known anyone to treat her unfairly because of her family's origins. But then, there was no way that someone could know from looking at her that she was Senemi. Her family didn't wear any of the traditional styles of the Onami. Why would they, since they were Senemi? They'd chosen to live in the city and leave the caravans. That was what made them Senemi, and not Onami, in their culture.

"We need to be careful," her ma had said. Would helping Lyria find her magic case count as being careful? Kev bit her lip. She had a feeling it wouldn't. But the damage had been done; Ferra had already told Lyria about Kev's sketches. Perhaps she would have to tell them she couldn't help. Except, Kev wanted to know what had happened to Lyria's case. She would just tell them not to tell anyone about her sketches. Lyria would understand, since she was Onami.

Now that she had drawn for a bit, Kev could return to her reading for school. She put her sketchbook and pencils away and settled back in her bed to read. Green Bean and Turnip, who had been playing and eating in their cage, came over to the bed and settled themselves in the blankets alongside Kev. She stroked her hand along their backs and smiled.

"We'll need to be careful about you, too," she said to them. Their noses twitched in her direction as if they were listening to her speak. They probably were, she thought. "But I guess you're already pretty good at that."

FLOWERMILLER CAFE

In the morning, Kev woke early to help her ma pack up her cart. Every year, Kev's mother hired a small cart and a mule from the dockyards to bring her things to the fair. Every year the Onami caravan traveled down from their summer journeys in the north and paused at the fairgrounds north of Mirella to trade goods, stories, and songs. People from Mirella, like Kev's ma, came to the fairgrounds with their own wares and set up shop too. Many farmers and artisans from farther out of the city even packed up their own wagons and camped alongside the Onami for the duration of the fair.

Kev helped her ma fill the cart outside the garden gate, bringing baskets, crates, and bags from the work tables and arranging them carefully in the little cart. It was just big enough to hold the day's worth of yarn, dyes, and seeds that her mother would sell. Her mother would walk alongside the cart.

Since the Scholar's Tower lay between Kev's house and the fairground, Kev and her ma walked together up one of the main roads up the hill. A crisp autumn breeze kept them cool under the bright sun as they led the donkey along.

They had almost reached the Scholar's Tower when a mage-driven cart thundered through a crossroads and nearly hit the donkey. The donkey reared, and bags toppled out of the back of Ma's cart. The mage-driven cart, powered by magic with not a horse to be seen, had swerved to avoid the donkey but in turn managed to clip the side of a food vending stand.

While Kev steadied the mule, her ma marched up to the mage, who had stepped out of his cart to pay the vendor. Kev winced at her ma's determined stance. She would not want to be the mage.

"How dare you drive your cart so recklessly!" Ma said, glaring at the mage with her hands on her hips. "You could have injured my mule."

The mage turned from the food seller and looked Kev's ma up and down, then gave a brief glance to Kev and the cart. Kev grabbed the last few bags from the ground and finished packing them back into nooks and crannies on the cart.

"Yet the mule appears unscathed," the mage said in a monotone voice. He reached into his purse and withdrew a coin. "Take this, it should be sufficient for your trouble."

Kev's ma kept her hands on her hips.

"I don't need that," she snapped. "I need your mage number."

A curtain in the window of the carriage was snatched open and a boy's face appeared.

"Radelm, what is taking so long?"

Kev scowled when she saw who it was. Tanar. Another face appeared beside his, and Kev recognized his merchant friend from class, Yeran.

"This fine lady has requested my mage number," the mage said in his same monotone.

"Just give her a coin and let's be on our way," Tanar said with annoyance.

"She won't take coin," the mage said.

Tanar rolled his eyes.

"Then give her the number and let's go."

The mage's lip curled slightly as he glanced sideways at Tanar, then turned to the front of the carriage and took out a box from under his seat. Without another word, he handed a card to Kev's ma, then turned his back to her and mounted his seat in the carriage.

Yeran's eyes lighted on Kev and he laughed and nudged Tanar with his shoulder. He pointed to Kev and Tanar's eyes followed. When Tanar saw Kev, he rolled his eyes and turned dramatically away from the window. He said something that Kev couldn't hear, and both boys laughed. The curtain on the window closed as the laughter continued. The carriage drove off.

Kev felt her cheeks flush and she frowned. She didn't care what Tanar and his friend thought of her. Nevertheless, their behavior towards her made her angry.

Kev's ma stalked back to their cart, the card gripped in her hand and her eyes glittering with anger.

"Some mages think they're more important than anyone else who walks the street," she said as she checked over the donkey. "Just because they're driving some merchant's child about the city." She glared up the road in the direction the cart had gone.

"The boys in the carriage are in my classes at the Scholar's Tower," Kev said.

"Oh? Then you can tell them to ask their mage to take more care," said her mother.

Kev just laughed. "From what I know of them, I doubt that would go over very well."

"Just as well as my conversation with the mage went, I suppose," Ma said with a sigh.

"Yeah, probably a lot like that," Kev agreed.

As Ma took the reins to lead the mule once more, she glanced over her shoulder at the cart. Kev was standing beside it now, having secured all of the loose bags that she'd returned to it.

"Oh, I didn't realize you had the rats along," Ma said.

"What?" Kev turned around to find Turnip and Green Bean perched atop the goods in the cart looking like royalty on a soft cotton sack full of yarn. Their noses waved in the air, taking in the scents around them.

"How did you get here?" Kev squeaked. She turned to her ma. "I didn't bring them. They just keep following me!"

Ma laughed and patted the rats. "Well, maybe you two would rather come with me to the fair today. Lots of good things to eat there," she said. "And lots of space to explore."

"It's true," Kev said, nodding intently at the rats. She tossed an empty sack over them. "And try not to be seen out here, either. The shopkeepers won't appreciate seeing rats."

"All right," said Ma, patting the mule's neck, "here we go again."

The rest of their walk up the hill was uneventful, and Kev arrived at the Scholar's Tower with plenty of time before her first class. She bade her ma goodbye and checked the cart to see that the rats were still in there. Even so, she couldn't rule out the possibility that they'd turn up in her school bag later.

As the cart trundled away up the hill in the direction of the Outpost, Kev turned to the gates of the low wall that bordered the small stretch of gardens and lawn in front of the school. She was glad she didn't have any classes with Tanar today; she didn't know how she would react to his insult, and she hoped he wouldn't have anything to say to her.

After her first two classes of the morning, Kev had a long stretch of time for lunch and study. It was during this time that she'd agreed to go to the cafe with Ferra and Lyria. She was supposed to meet them at the library in the arts wing of the Tower.

Since Kev was a new student, she was mostly taking general classes, and hadn't chosen a specialty yet. So, she had not been to the arts wing except for on a tour she'd taken during the summer, after she'd passed her entrance exam.

Although it was called the arts wing, it was actually more its own building. The Scholar's Tower itself was a collection of buildings that seemed to have grown out from each other organically, like a collection of mushrooms. At some point, it had been just a tower, and gotten its name, but by now it was no longer even clear which of the buildings might have been the original tower, because there were several candidates.

One of those candidates was the tower on the arts wing building, and as luck would have it, the tower was now the arts wing library.

Unlike other libraries on the Scholar's Tower grounds, the arts wing library was a somewhat bustling place. The first floor was the most like other libraries, with its walls stacked with shelves full of books and tables in the middle of the room where students worked alone or in whispering groups.

But as Kev ascended through the floors to the fourth floor where she was to meet her friends, she passed work rooms full of chattering students, supply shelves haphazardly stacked with paints, clay, dyes, fabric, and more, and open floors of comfortable seating with groups of students lounging throughout.

The fourth floor was a bit quieter and more serene than the last two Kev had passed through. One half of the floor was taken up by rows of bookshelves, and the other half held tables and work benches. The work benches were pushed against the wall on one side and stuck out into the room, so that each student had a little work area. Each work bench was backed by a tall board that bore shelves, pegs, and drawers. In addition to storage space, the back board provided privacy and a quiet nook for the students to work in.

Kev found Ferra and Lyria at one of these work benches. The drawers were pulled out, and tools were scattered all around Lyria as she bent over a cloth spread out on the table before her. Lyria bit her bottom lip as she held a small pliers in one hand and twisted a fine wire around it in the other hand. Her hand dropped to a pile of small stone beads on the cloth before her, she placed one on the wire, then picked up the pliers again and gave the wire a twist to secure the bead in place.

The effect was like a tree, or a many-petaled flower twining elegantly about the main stem of wires twisted together.

"That's beautiful," Kev said as she approached the bench. "What do you make with it? A necklace?"

Lyria flinched and looked up, startled. She smiled at Kev and looked down at the wire and bead creation in her hands.

"Oh, I don't know yet. It's just something to help me think. It keeps my hands busy."

Ferra looked up from the book she'd been reading with a smile.

"Kev! It must be time to go to Flowermiller Cafe!" She closed her book and packed it in her bag. "That's great, because I was getting tired of reading about the elements of magic. I'll never be able to see them myself anyway. Good to know, but it's a long read."

"I'll be ready in a moment," said Lyria. "Just let me finish this part up, and then I'll pack up."

Lyria did a few more wraps on her wire creation and then carefully folded it up in the felt pad she'd lain out to work on. She scooped the pile of beads into a little pouch and stacked the tools back into their drawers. She packed her project and supplies into her satchel, and then locked the drawers and cabinets at the work station with a key that was tied to a long carved and pointed wand.

"All right, just have to return my key," Lyria said, holding up the wand with a smile.

Kev and Ferra followed her to the desk near the front door of the room, where a young man, maybe another student, sat hunched over a book. he looked up as they approached and smiled at Lyria. She held out her key.

"Thank you, Dinnan," she said. "See you tomorrow, probably."

"I'll be here," Dinnan replied. He placed a bookmark and closed his book before turning away from the counter to hang the key on its rightful hook on the wall behind him. The wand that the key was attached to hung among several other wands, all decorated in their own styles.

Kev followed Ferra and Lyria out the door of the library, and then out of the arts wing through a different door than the one through which she'd entered. They took a narrow staircase that hugged the curved walls of the tower down to a set of doors that opened to a small brick-paved courtyard surrounded by Scholar's Tower buildings. A large tree in the middle of the courtyard stretched its branches up high above the tower, its leaves providing shade from the bright autumn sun. Dapples of sunlight danced over the bricks as a light breeze rustled through the leaves.

"I didn't even know this was here," Kev said. "It's so pretty."

Lyria smiled. "It's one of my favorite spots," she said. She pointed across the courtyard to where the corners of two buildings met. "We can go through there to get to the cafe."

They passed by benches occupied by other students chatting quietly or reading, then slipped through the passage to emerge onto a bright, busy side street. Kev didn't recognize where they were until they turned from the side street onto a larger thoroughfare, Trade Street, which ran up the hill toward the north. Just off Trade Street, they turned off into a square and came to Flowermiller Cafe.

Kev had never been to Flowermiller Cafe before, though she had known it was popular with students at the Scholar's Tower for treats and studying. Today, with the nice weather, wooden tables dotted the square in front of the cafe, shaded by a canvas awning that stretched out from the building. The front door was propped open, and Kev could smell the scents of sweet things baking. She followed Ferra and Lyria through the open door and to the counter, where they ordered spiced cakes and tea from a tall, stocky woman with a cheery smile.

"Thank you dearies," said the lady as she took their coin. "Amara will have your things at the counter." She tipped her head to the left, indicating a long wooden counter where a younger girl worked, pulling the cakes from baskets on shelves behind them and assembling a wooden tray with their teas.

"That's Mistress Flowermiller," Lyria whispered as they

moved down toward the end counter to wait. "She owns the cafe."

Past the counter was an open room with plenty of tables, and along one wall was a row of booths. At the back of the room, a counter was lined with taller stools. In the front, wide windows were opened to let the daylight in, and a door at one side allowed passage to the outdoor seating.

"Where were you sitting when your case was stolen?" Ferra asked. "We should sit in the same spot."

"Does it matter?" Lyria said with a frown.

Ferra looked to Kev. "Do you think it helps?" she asked.

"I don't know," said Kev. "I guess it couldn't hurt." She lowered her voice and leaned in toward Ferra. "It's not like I've done this before. Not on purpose, like this."

"Oh. Right," said Ferra.

"It was here," Lyria said when they reached a table in the corner next to the front window. She set their tray down, then eased her bag off her shoulder and set it between her feet.

Kev and Ferra followed suit and took chairs as well. Ferra helped herself to some tea and her cake, and then poured a cup and set it in front of Kev.

"So," Ferra said after she had finished a bite of her spiced cake. "Tell us about that day. What do you remember? Who was here? Were there a lot of people at the tables around you?"

Lyria frowned in the face of Ferra's eager questions. She chewed slowly as she gazed around the room, which was currently fairly empty, it seemed to Kev.

"I don't know; I don't think I was paying that much attention," Lyria said after she had washed down her cake with a sip of tea. She cradled the cup in her hands. "Um, Mistress Flowermiller was here," she said.

Ferra had pulled out sheaf of paper and made a note. Then she looked eagerly back up at Lyria. "All right, that's a start. Who else?"

"Well, lots of people were here, Ferra!" Lyria said. "How am I supposed to remember people I don't even know?"

Ferra slumped back and sighed. "I just meant like, if you remembered anyone strange, or if somebody was doing something strange."

"No..." Lyria trailed off. "I just don't look around that much," she said. Then she sighed. "Ferra, how is this supposed to help me find my jeweler's case? It was probably just some purse stealer who saw a good chance and took it."

"But the hot bead! There has to be more to that!" Ferra said. "And that's why Kev's here, remember?"

Both other girls looked to Kev expectantly, and Kev flinched.

Kev had been eating her cake as she listened to Ferra and Lyria talk. It seemed like they wanted her to say something now, but like Lyria, she was a bit at a loss.

"I can try to draw something," Kev offered. "I can't promise anything, but I'll try."

"Will you do it now?" Ferra asked.

"Yes, of course," Kev said. She reached into her satchel for her sketchbook and special pencils, which she'd packed today in anticipation of this visit. Like Lyria, she hadn't thought much about what they would actually do once they arrived here at the cafe. In the past, she had never deliberately tried to draw something to find something out like this, not really. It had been more intuitive when she'd done it to find the weyrdragon last spring, and she hadn't even known it would work.

She would have to make a mental note to Ferra not to offer up her services to anybody else. It wasn't as if she was a mage who could just set herself to her scrying bowl any time she wanted.

With paper and pencils before her, Kev looked around the room for somewhere to start. She started to sketch a table in the foreground. Ferra and Lyria looked on with interest; they weren't even sipping their tea anymore. As Kev finished the beginning outline of the table and moved on to the serving counters in the background, she began to feel the weight of her friends' gazes on her. Her hand shook a little and she pulled it back to her lap.

Ferra made a face at the paper. "That doesn't tell us much, does it?"

"It's not finished!" Kev snapped. She closed her sketchbook. "I'm sorry, I can't do this." She looked to Lyria. "I'm sorry, I hope you can find your jeweler's case. I wish I could help." She bundled her sketchbook and pencils up in her arms and with another "I'm sorry," she fled the Flowermiller Cafe.

Rat Training

After classes, Kev's head swirled with what had happened at the cafe. She walked home with her head down, arms still wrapped around her sketchbook. A pit formed in her stomach thinking about how she had stormed out on Ferra and Lyria. She shouldn't have reacted that way; she wished she could have been calmer. But why did Ferra have to tell Lyria about her sketches, and make her think that Kev was some expert who knew how to find a lost bag? A lost bag, of all things! As Lyria had said, it was probably just a purse snatcher who had seen the right moment to whisk it away from her while she was distracted.

Although the bead that had burned her *was* intriguing, Kev had to admit. Then she scowled. That still didn't mean she could do anything about it.

A shadow passed overhead and Kev looked up. It was a dragon flying low over the city, gliding by on glittering wings. She admired the way the afternoon autumn sunlight hit the golden pattern of its scales. Perhaps it was a dragon she knew, she thought, smiling to herself. She was a person who knew dragons, now. Even though it had taken awhile for dragons in general to grow on her, Kev couldn't help but feel a little special to be well acquainted with some of the dragon riders at the outpost. Eldet's ma, Dynet, had a dragon with golden scales.

At that thought, Kev stopped in her tracks. Eldet. Eldet was supposed to come to her house today after classes. She groaned. It wasn't "perhaps" a dragon she knew, it was a dragon she knew! Eldet's ma was flying him to her house. Of all the days to have a fight (was it a fight?) with Ferra.

Kev picked up her pace and tried to put thoughts of the Flowermiller Cafe out of her mind.

As she got closer to home, she could hear the commotion caused by the dragon landing in the square outside her family's front door. It wasn't common for dragons to descend into the middle of the city very often, since their wings tended to get cramped between buildings on many of the streets. So whenever dragons showed up outside Kev's home, she'd learned to expect a crowd.

Eldet was just sliding down from Riki's back when Kev reached the square, and he gave her a big smile and a wave. Then he turned and waved to his ma, who remained on dragonback. Riki pumped his wings gently a few times in warning to the people who had drawn close, then began to beat them harder as he lifted off into the air again.

The people who'd gathered to stare at the dragon now turned their stares toward Eldet, whose cheeks were red. He gave them a bashful wave and rubbed a hand through his hair.

"Sorry for all the commotion," he said to Kev. "Ma didn't want me to be late, and she said she was going out on patrol anyway."

"My neighbors will probably get used to it eventually," Kev said. It had only been a few months since she'd become friends with Eldet, and by extension, his ma and their other dragon rider friends. "Anyway, it gives them something to talk about. Adds some excitement to the neighborhood."

Eldet laughed. "I never realized it was such an excitement to see dragons until I started coming here. I thought everybody was used to them."

"Not used to being this close," Kev said. Of course to Eldet, dragons were no big excitement. He'd grown up as the son of a dragon rider and had lived at the dragon Outpost all his life until last year, when he'd been sent to live with his uncle in the city of Areth so he could study at the main Mage Academy.

Eldet's time in Areth hadn't worked out quite as well as his ma had hoped. His interest in magical creatures led to him being kidnapped by creature sellers and smuggled back to Mirella, chasing after a fire breathing miniature dragon called a weyr-dragon. So, Eldet now lived at the Outpost with his Ma and sister again and studied at the branch of the Mage Academy here in Mirella. He had finally won permission to put his mage skills to use in studying creatures—magical or not—and was now apprenticed under an expert creature mage in addition to his regular studies.

Kev had met Eldet during his kidnapping ordeal with the weyr-dragon in the spring, when she and Ferra had been searching for him and managed to get themselves imprisoned as well. He'd also met Kev's rats at the same time, and now he was especially fond of the creatures, as well as quite curious. They'd first shown their uncanny intelligence and magical abilities to Kev when they'd helped her and her friends escape from Lady Orsta, the illegal creature collector who had wanted the weyrdragon. Eldet had been fascinated by the rats ever since. So now, whenever he could, he came to study them and try different training tricks that he had learned in his apprenticeship.

Kev and Eldet entered the house, where they found her father making dinner and her siblings seated in various locations around the front room, either reading or working on their own school-work. Sayess, her six-year-old sister, rolled over from where she lay on her stomach in front of the hearth and waved at Kev. Her face brightened when she saw Eldet too.

"Are there dragons outside?"

"Already gone," said Jaen from the table, not even looking up from the paper he was hunched over, writing.

"Why didn't you tell me?" Sayess whined.

"You're supposed to be reading," Jaen said with a shrug.

"Is Ma home yet?" Kev asked, just now remembering that the rats had accompanied Ma to the market again. Seemingly, they had liked their trip with her the day before.

"Not too much longer," said Da. "What do you need?"

"The rats, actually," Kev said. "It's okay though, we can wait." She turned to Eldet. "You know how I said the rats have been showing up in all kinds of places?"

As they ascended the stairs to her room, she explained to Eldet about the rats' recent trip to the fair with her Ma.

When she opened the door, though, she was surprised to find Turnip and Green Bean both curled up in a sweater that she had thrown on her bed. They yawned and stretched their little arms out, only their heads showing from within the folds of knitted wool. Kev laughed and went to the bed to pet them. They squirmed out of their warm nest and allowed Kev to pick them up. She held Turnip out to Eldet, who smiled and let the rat walk onto his arm.

"Guess they got tired of the fair," Eldet said, smiling as he stroked the top of Turnip's head. "Now how did you get home, I wonder?" He looked down at Turnip as he asked the question, and she sniffed her nose in his direction.

Kev shook her head. "I wish I knew. Do you think they can disappear and reappear places? Can mages make animals do that? Can *mages* do that?"

Eldet scrunched up his face in thought. "I don't know. Maybe they could make a portal, or hide from sight. But maybe I just haven't learned of it yet. Some of the more advanced stuff, mages don't like to talk about to just anyone, you know? You've never seen the rats do it?"

"No, they just turn up in my bag, or my ma's cart the other day. Anywhere but their cage," Kev said, holding up Green Bean so she could give her a pointed stare.

Green Bean backed out of Kev's hands and dropped to her lap, then began to wander around the bed.

Eldet set Turnip in his lap and drew a small paper packet out of his pocket. At the sound of the crinkling paper, both rats immediately ran to his hands and started pulling on his fingers with their tiny little paws.

"Oho, you can tell that's for you, can you?" Eldet said with a laugh. He pulled his hands away from the scrabbling rats and unfolded the top of the packet. He pulled out two small brown balls of something that looked like bread and gave one to each rat. They took their treats and raced to their cage, where they each found a hiding spot and nibbled furiously.

"There's more where that came from," Eldet called after them. "If you help me with my experiments," he added. He tucked the paper pouch back into his pocket and kept his arm over it so that when the rats returned, they would not be able to dig in his pocket and help themselves to more treats.

"What were those?" Kev asked. She was used to the rats' excitement over all kinds of food, but they had seemed even more excited than usual for Eldet's treats.

"Little fish biscuits, sort of," he answered. "The cooks at the Outpost let me take some of the dough when they were making them last. Riders bring them on long patrols because they keep well. I remember my ma saying that she's often had troubles keeping mice out of her pack when the fish biscuits are in there."

Green Bean and Turnip returned to the door of the cage once they had finished their treats and peered at Eldet, clearly hoping that he would hand them another treat so they could go right back to their hiding places and nibble on them again.

"Now, are you ready to learn some tricks?" Eldet asked them. "Then you can earn another one."

"What are you going to teach them this time?" Kev asked. At a previous visit, Eldet had attempted to teach the rats simple tricks, like putting a small wooden ball into a jar, or running through a tiny obstacle course he'd constructed for them on the floor. However, his simple tricks, which he said took normal rats days to learn, with many steps building up to the final sequence, only took Green Bean and Turnip a few minutes to master.

"Master Rithorn helped me come up with some harder ones," Eldet said. "But he was pleased with my notes about the first set of tricks too."

Master Rithorn was the creature mage who Eldet had been apprenticed to. Kev knew that in the past, Eldet had been actively discouraged from his interest in animals in favor of his mage training, but now that he was able to combine the two interests, he seemed very happy whenever Kev saw him.

Eldet took a notebook out of his pack and flipped to a page full of writing and drawings. He consulted it and then began to talk earnestly to the rats as if they could understand everything he said. Kev did it too, talking to them like that, but she never really knew for sure whether they understood her, or if they just seemed to sometimes.

It seemed that Eldet had the same thoughts regarding their understanding of language, because the "tricks" that he began to test them on all required that they understand verbal instructions. Unlike the fetching and carrying tricks they had picked up so quickly before, where he led them around with a treat in his hand, now he refrained from gesturing at all.

He set several colored wooden blocks out in a row in front of him, then scooped Green Bean from where she sniffled near his pocket. He set her on the floor with the row of blocks between them.

"Now, Green Bean, you will get a treat if you can bring me the correct block three times. All right?"

Green Bean had begun to groom herself as Eldet spoke, seemingly oblivious to what he had said. Now Turnip was the one scrabbling at his treat pocket. Eldet gently removed her and set her in his lap.

"You'll get your turn too, Turnip. Don't worry."

Turnip climbed onto his arm and scaled his sleeve up to his shoulder, then settled there under his ear.

"Thank you for your patience," Eldet said with a grin. "Now, Green Bean, your first task. Can you bring me the purple block?"

Green Bean paused her grooming and actually seemed to be thinking about it. Then she came forward toward the blocks, picked up the red one, and brought it to Eldet's hand. She stood on her hind legs and looked up at him as if to ask, "Do I get my treat now?"

Eldet's shoulders slumped.

"I don't know what to do with that," he said. "Does she understand, because she brought me a block, or does she not, because she brought me the wrong color?"

Kev laughed. "And how long will she keep bringing you blocks before she quits because she hasn't gotten a treat yet?"

"Well, I'll try it a few more times. Maybe I need to teach them the color names first."

Eldet continued to set out blocks and talk with the rats quietly, and Kev took her books out to get started on that night's reading. After reading awhile, her mind began to wander to the cafe and Lyria's stolen case again. When Eldet's work with the rats seemed to come to a pause, she spoke her thoughts out loud.

"What kind of magic could make a stone bead burn?"

At Eldet's puzzled look, she explained what had happened to Lyria, and how Ferra had asked her to help. She also sheepishly described how she had walked out on Ferra and Lyria that day.

"But I don't even know how to help!" she finished.

"What about the rats?" Eldet said brightly.

"What?"

"They've helped you before, haven't they? They helped you find me!" Eldet said. "Didn't you?" he crooned to the two rats who now sat cradled in his lap enjoying their latest fish biscuit treat.

"True, but I don't know how to get them to do anything like that, they just did it all on their own." Then she giggled. "And, it seems like they can't even tell the difference between a yellow block and a green block. Even if I knew how I wanted them to help, how would I tell them?"

At that comment, Green Bean and Turnip left Eldet's lap and scampered over to the pile of blocks, which had been pushed off to the side as Eldet had gotten increasingly discouraged with the outcomes of his experiments. Green Bean picked up a yellow block, and Turnip picked up a green block. They carried their blocks over to Kev and deposited them on her lap.

Eldet gaped. "You cheeky weasels!" he exclaimed as the rats climbed to Kev's shoulders and nuzzled her neck. "They were fooling me!" Then his expression changed from consternation to thoughtfulness and he reached for his notebook and pencil and started to write.

"I wish they could talk to us," Eldet said. "They must understand so much more than I thought." He pursed his lips and stared at the rats again. "And we don't even know where they came from. Maybe someday I'll try to find out what mage raised them." He trailed off and he scribbled another note, lips still pursed.

Kev reached up to stroke Turnip with her right hand. When she looked back to Eldet, she flinched. He was grinning at her widely, a look she did not like.

"Why do I have the feeling you're about to say something that could get me into trouble?"

"I can help you with the rats, to help you find Ferra's friend's craft case! It'll be the perfect chance for me to study their abilities!" Eldet said. "And it'll be like, a chance for me to repay you for finding me at Lady Orsta's."

"That was a one-time thing," Kev said. "And you don't need to repay me anything." Green Bean chose that moment to start climbing down from Kev's shoulder, so Kev held out her arm to make a little ramp. Green Bean landed in her lap, then went straight to Eldet to try getting into his pocket again. Absently,

Eldet lifted the flap over the top of his pocket and let Green Bean climb in.

"What if it keeps them busy?" he said. "It will give them something to do while you're in school. No more popping up in your satchel at unexpected times!" Eldet said cheerfully.

"You can't guarantee that won't still happen," Kev said with a roll of her eyes. "But you might have a point there." She scooped Turnip off of her other shoulder and held the rat up to her face. "What do you think? Do you want to help us find some lost craft supplies? And some jewelry too?"

In answer, Turnip squirmed out of her hands and made her way over to Eldet's lap next to Green Bean, where she quickly helped herself to more of the fish biscuit treats from his pocket.

"I think they're saying they'll help as long as I continue to provide the treats," Eldet said with a laugh. Then his expression grew more serious.

"As for your sketching," he said, "I think the cafe was the wrong place to try drawing her case. Or whatever you need to draw to try to find it."

Kev looked at him in surprise. Once he'd gotten onto the topic of the rats helping her search for Lyria's case, she figured he'd forgotten her original question.

"I mean, when I'm working magic, I can't just do it anywhere," Eldet said. "I haven't trained long enough for that. Magic takes concentration and practice. That's easier in a quiet place."

"I don't even know if what I have is magic," Kev whispered, reluctant to let her family overhear. Her ma and da were familiar with the role her sketches had played in Kev's adventures this spring, but she talked about it as little as possible in front of her siblings, just in case they got any crazy ideas.

Eldet waved off her concern. "Whatever you want to call it, I just think you might have an easier time sketching by yourself, and then if you get results, bring them to Ferra later." He shrugged. "That's what I would do, anyway. Oh, and probably apologize to Ferra and her friend."

Kev threw her sweater at Eldet and he blocked it, laughing.

"Of course I'll apologize," she said, rolling her eyes.

A few moments later, Kev's da called up the stairs for dinner, so they returned the rats to their cage and headed down to the supper table.

"Where's Ma?" Kev asked when she reached the table, seeing that she wasn't there.

"I'm sure she'll be here soon," said Da. "She probably got caught up with some of her cousins and lost track of the time." As he said it, he glanced out the window where the afternoon light was fading.

Kev and Eldet took bowls from the counter and served themselves stew from the pot on the stove in addition to thick slices of bread with butter.

As dinner went on, Kev's da sent increasingly worried glances toward the front door and out the window. Although the Onami fair was busy and full of opportunities for trade, it wasn't like Ma to stay too late. She didn't like to miss dinner, and she didn't like to have to handle her wagon in the dark.

Finally, Da went to the door and stepped outside, peering up the street in the direction of the market. He came back in shortly and shook his head. Kev and her siblings exchanged glances.

"When my ma comes to get me, I could ask her if we could fly to the market to look for her," Eldet said.

"Thank you, Eldet," said Da with a sigh. "I hope we won't have to take you up on that."

To everyone's surprise, when Eldet's ma arrived on Riki's back in the square outside their house, Kev's ma was already with her. The whole family spilled out into the square as the two women slid down from the dragon's back.

Ma smiled as her children ran to embrace her. Eldet moved to help Dynet remove several packs from the back of the dragon.

"I'm so sorry I'm late," Ma said. "There was quite a commotion at the fair, and I got stuck. Thank you," she added as she accepted her packs from Eldet and Dynet. "I had to leave the cart and the mule with my cousin Kalla. I'll be able to get them back tomorrow."

Kev's da moved to Ma's side after Kev's younger siblings had all gotten their hugs. He put an arm around her shoulders. "Come inside, you can tell us after you've had something to eat." He looked to Dynet. "Would you like any stew?"

"Thank you, but I'll need to return to the fair after I've brought Eldet home. I'm still on patrol for another few hours, and the happenings at the fair will require our attention."

"What happened?" asked Kadan, who had moved on to stroking Riki's side after he'd finished greeting Ma.

Ma sighed and frowned. "Several of the artisans had their things stolen. Not only their wares, but their tools, too."

Eldet's eyes widened and he looked at Kev. Kev gaped back at him.

"What kinds of things?" she asked her ma. "What kind of artisans were stolen from?"

"All kinds," Ma said. "My cousin Vansal, the herbalist, had a case full of his tools stolen, along with many of his herbs for sale. That's why I was stuck there so long. But we heard of others, leatherworkers, painters, embroiderers, a weaver even had a small loom stolen."

"Come inside and tell us while you eat," Da said. "Thank you for bringing her home, Dynet."

Dynet nodded and motioned for Eldet to join her on Riki's back.

"Just a minute," Eldet said, and took Kev aside as the rest of her family filed back into the house.

"Tell me the next time you meet with Ferra and Lyria," he said. "I want to help, not just because of the rats. And I think we need to go to the fair."

"I'll talk to her tomorrow. If there's time, we'll come to the Outpost," Kev agreed.

"Bring the rats," Eldet said as he took his ma's hand and climbed into the saddle on Riki's back.

"I'm sure the rats will show up whether I ask them to or not," Kev answered with a grin.

She stayed in the square outside her door while Riki flapped his wings and took off, the wind scattering dust and leaves to the walls.

This had just gotten a lot bigger than Lyria's crafting case.

SKETCHMAGIC

The next morning, Kev woke early so she could do some sketching before she set out for her classes. Ma had recounted more about the incidents at the fair while she finished her dinner, but it had soon grown late, and Ma was tired. From the bits of information that her mother had shared, Kev became more and more convinced that the thefts at the Onami fair were related to the theft of Lyria's project bag.

First, the theft that her mother knew the most about was her cousin Vansal's. Vansal and his wife Kalla both sold items they made at the fair. Vansal was an herbalist who cultivated plants and created all kinds of teas, tinctures, salves, and the like from the herbs he collected along their caravan's route each year. In fact, some of Ma's dye plants doubled as plants for Vansal's medicines, and she grew them and brought them to the fair each year in trade for some of Vansal's things in return.

Ma said that not long before Vansal noticed some of his jars missing, he had been working with his mortar and pestle at the back of their trading stall while he waited for folk to come buy his wares. Ma and Kalla were in the stall too, sitting a little off to the side and spinning wool on their spindles while they chatted and shared some tea. They had been startled from their spindling by

Vansal's cry, and turned to find him cursing over a pile of crushed herbs that had been scattered over his lap and the floor.

When Kalla went to help him pick up the mortar and pestle that he'd spilled, she quickly dropped the pestle with a few curses of her own. It was hot to the touch. Ma and her cousins looked everywhere around their stall for some explanation for the sudden warmth of the stone, but there was nothing. Stranger still, many of the dried plants that Vansal had spread out on the table next to his work looked charred, as if they had been burned as well. There had been no fire or smoke.

They were still trying to figure out what had happened when several groups of customers came to the stall, and they all stopped to help them. When they returned to the back shelves of the stall and the storage boxes below the table, Vansal found that several of his mortars and pestles, dried plants, jars, and cutting tools had disappeared. He and Kalla looked high and low, inside and outside of their wagon, but found nothing. Their children, teens who were older than Kev by several years, were out walking the markets selling flowers or visiting with their friends, so they were not seen until well after Vansal's things disappeared.

Before Vansal could report it all to the fair officials, there were sounds of outcry from several other nearby stalls, and a crowd began to form outside in the fairgrounds. That was when the dragon riders and mage guard had to be called in, and by then, Ma was required to stay and give her account of what had happened to the fair officials, the mage guard, and members of the dragon patrol. While she and her cousins were waiting, they managed to hear tales of thefts from at least five other sellers with stalls near theirs.

Kev took out the bracelet that Lyria had given her as a reference and rolled the stones in her fingers. Last night, she had wanted to tell her Ma of Lyria's project bag disappearing, especially with the heated bead being in common with cousin Vansal's burning tools. But she hadn't had a chance last night, and now she wondered if she should share about her work with Lyria yet.

Her ma might not like it if she knew Kev was trying to use her sketchmagic and sharing knowledge of its existence with others.

She sighed, thinking again about her fruitless quest to find more information about craftmagic in the Tower libraries. Well, even if she couldn't find anything more written down, she had another source of information: herself. She set Lyria's bracelet down on the windowsill where she could see it and picked up her sketchbook and pencil.

At first she just doodled for a while, easing into her practice. Since classes had started at the Scholar's Tower, she had not had as much time as usual to lose herself in her sketching as she often used to. Now, with plenty of time before breakfast, she let her mind wander as she sketched. She drew rough sketches of the rats pawing in Eldet's pockets, Riki flying out of the courtyard with two figures upon her back, and then her imaginings of a mortar and pestle on a table with bunches of dried herbs hanging from a string on the wall above.

With her drawing muscles warmed up, Kev now looked to the bracelet. She began by copying the object as she saw it in the windowsill, leaving plenty of space on the page around it to fill in more of the picture. She started with the polished stone beads, then added the knotted cord patterns around them, admiring Lyria's even tension and tidy tie-offs at the ends.

Almost without noticing, she shifted to drawing the table beneath the bracelet, the knotted wood grain of the sturdy oak tables, a plate with a half-finished pastry on it next to a mug of coffee. The picture was shown from the perspective Lyria would have had if she were sitting before it, working on her craft, so next came a small leather pouch of beading supplies. Kev imagined Lyria must use it to keep the items for her current working organized from the rest of her supplies when she carried her things around with her to work on it in places like the Flowermiller Cafe.

Once the table and all its accessories were done, Kev kept going to illustrate more cafe tables in the background, filled up the serving counter with servers standing behind it, and added vague sketches of patrons sitting at other tables. These figures were blurred and not quite filled out, but Kev managed to fit some detail in on a few of the faces closer to the table at the center of the image.

There. That was done. She smoothed the paper under her hands and closed her sketchbook. She would find Ferra at school today, show her the sketch, and tell her about the thefts at the Onami fair.

After breakfast, Kev walked together with her ma again on the way to the Scholar's Tower and the Onami Fair. Today, Ma wore a basket on her back full of some additional skeins of yarn and packets of seeds and dried dye plants. She would collect the wagon and mule while she was there. The rats peered happily out of the top of Ma's basket.

When they stopped in front of the Scholar's Tower to say goodbye, Kev asked the rats, "Would you like to come with me today? Eldet wants to see you after my classes. He'll probably bring more fish treats."

Whether they could understand her words or not, the rats climbed eagerly from the basket into Kev's arms and allowed her to place them in the soft pouch that she'd made for carrying them around. She tucked it inside her satchel so it would be concealed while she was in her classes.

Unfortunately, today she had History of Magic again, and when she arrived, Tanar was already in a seat, and he was glaring right at her. Mage Valaso hadn't arrived yet. Kev did her best to ignore Tanar's glare and chose a seat far away from him. What was he angry about now?

She didn't have to wonder for long, because as soon as she took her seat, Tanar was out of his, walking straight over to the seat in front of Kev's. He spun the chair in front of her around, sat on it, and leaned onto the table in front of her, blocking her from setting down the books she'd just taken from her satchel.

"What is your mother's name?" he said in a low, tense voice. "She owes me."

"She doesn't owe you anything," Kev said flatly. She didn't say more, knowing that for people like Tanar, the more she said, the more ammunition she would give him for whatever he was about to do. She set her books on the table anyway, next to Tanar's arms.

"I know it was her," he said. "She reported my mage driver to the licensing office and now he's suspended. For two months!" He slapped his open palm down hard on the table as he said it, and several students nearby flinched in their seats. Kev had flinched too, but she did her best to harden her expression.

"If you do that again," she said, pointing at Tanar's hand, "I will report you to Mage Valaso and the Tower scholars. And I will not be talking to you about my mother." She stood, took her books, and moved to a different seat without looking back at Tanar.

The legs of Tanar's chair squealed against the stone floor as he pushed himself up, and from the corner of Kev's eyes, she could see that he was about to follow her. At that moment, Mage Valaso entered the room from the door at the front and began to arrange his books on the podium. He smiled out at the class and greeted them cheerfully, bidding them to have a seat.

Tanar went back to his seat as the lecture began, and Kev stared at the back of his head while he leaned close to Yeran and seemed to continue his angry rant. The two boys were soon smiling, and Tanar's friend glanced back at Kev, said something to Tanar, and they both laughed.

Mage Valaso cleared his throat and gave the boys a pointed stare. They controlled themselves, but Kev would have been oblivious if she did not notice several more glances over their shoulders in her direction throughout the rest of the lecture. She did her best to focus on Mage Valaso's words, and when he finished his lecture, she exited the room as quickly as she could to avoid another encounter.

"Merchants," she said under her breath and rolled her eyes as she saw Tanar and his friend leave the classroom and go down a different hall than the one she had chosen. She hoped that he would get over his misplaced anger, but she feared that he would not. This would not be good.

Luckily, the rest of her classes that day were much less eventful, and Kev never ran into Tanar again. During the break after her two morning classes, she took the rats to the sunny little courtyard near the arts wing that Lyria had shown her yesterday. Kev settled down under a tree and invited the rats out of their carry pouch so they could explore and do their business. She gave them a few pieces of biscuits and jam that she'd packed along as a snack.

It wasn't long before Lyria and Ferra showed up in the courtyard, as Kev had hoped they would. They looked unsure when they saw Kev, but she gave them a smile and a wave, so they came to sit by her.

"I'm sorry about yesterday," Kev said. "I didn't mean to be so snappish."

"I'm sorry too," Ferra said. "You were right, I was pushing you too hard with your sketches. I understand if you can't help in the way I thought you could."

"I can still help," Kev said with a smile. "And I've got something for you."

She showed them her sketchbook turned to the page with her drawing from this morning. Lyria took it and looked it over. She touched the page wonderingly.

"Did you go back to the cafe? This is exactly right!" she said. "It's like being there again."

"Here's this back," Kev said, handing Lyria the bracelet. "It was very useful."

"Oh no, please keep it," Lyria said, barely glancing up. Her eyes were still on the page. "Oh look, it's Dinnan." She pointed at one of the figures at the tables in the cafe picture. She didn't seem surprised.

"Who's Dinnan?" Kev asked.

"He works at the desk in the art library," Lyria said. "You would have seen him yesterday."

Now that she said it, Kev remembered the young man who had checked in Lyria's key when she returned it.

"Maybe I could ask him if he saw something," Lyria said with a smile. "He's always so friendly. And he lives in rooms above the Flowermiller Cafe, so maybe he's seen even more!" Then she frowned. "Although, I hope nobody else has had their things stolen at the cafe."

"I mean, he might not have been there on that day," Kev said. "It might be that his face just came to my mind while I was drawing and he ended up in my picture."

"Maybe," said Ferra, "but there's only one way to find out."

"What do you mean?" asked Kev, not liking the half grin on Ferra's lips.

"We have to go talk to Dinnan!"

Ferra looked like she was about to leap up that minute, but Kev put a hand on her arm.

"There's more I have to tell you," Kev said. "I think you were right, about this not being just a purse snatcher."

"I knew it!" Ferra said. "Wait, why do you say that?"

"Because more things have been stolen, at the Onami fair yesterday."

She told her friends all that her mother had relayed to her the night before, including her cousin Vansal's mortar and pestle seeming to burn.

"So I wonder if you should report your bag being stolen to the mage guard," Kev finished. "Since they're looking into these thefts from the fair, too."

Lyria looked uncomfortable at Kev's suggestion. "I'm—I don't want to get in trouble," she said.

"What for?" Kev asked.

"Remember I said my bag had a protection on it?"

Kev nodded. She did remember, and she remembered wondering what exactly Lyria had meant by that.

Lyria quickly glanced around the courtyard, as if making sure nobody was nearby to overhear her. Then she said quietly, "It's a magic protection that my friend put on it. She made the bag, and she makes them specially so the owners can't lose them or damage them, things like that. I don't know how strong it is against outright stealing, though. But I don't want to get her in trouble. The mage guard will think it's bound magic. They've taken Onami away for that before."

"They couldn't know that it had the protection on it though, when you just report it, right?" Kev said.

Lyria shrugged. "If they find it? I don't know." Then she slumped. "It's probably not ever going to get found anyway," she said.

"Not if we don't try," said Ferra. "Let's go talk to Dinnan."

"Wait, I still have more to say," Kev said, putting a hand on Ferra's arm again. "Eldet wants to help too. With the rats."

Ferra's eyes widened and her grin grew. She clapped her hands. "That's a perfect idea!" she said. Then she beckoned to the rats, who had taken up residence in Kev's lap. Green Bean uncurled and climbed into Ferra's outstretched hand. Ferra held Green Bean up to her, face to face.

"Are you going to help us find Lyria's jewelry case? You're a good rat, yes you are," she said in a baby voice. In answer, Green Bean licked her nose. Ferra giggled and cuddled Green Bean in her arms.

"Okay, *now* can we go talk to Dinnan?" Ferra asked.

Kev held out the rats' carry pouch. "I'll need my rat back, please."

As the three girls stood, Lyria's expression still looked a little pained.

"What's the matter?" Ferra asked.

"When we talk to Dinnan, make sure not to mention the protection on the bag, okay?" Lyria said.

"And while we're at it, don't mention my drawings." Kev added. "Maybe we can just ask him if he knows of anything happening in the cafe lately, with pickpockets and the like."

"I haven't told anyone about that besides Lyria," Ferra said.

"It's too hard to explain anyway, and people wouldn't believe it. Don't worry."

"Thanks," Kev said. She looked down at the rats inside her satchel. "Are you ready?" Their whiskered noses twitched back up at her from where they'd curled up together against the soft fleece fabric.

"All right," said Lyria, looking more confident now. "Let's go."

THE ONAMI FAIR

Dinnan was not in the library when the Kev and her friends arrived looking for him. A girl working at the front desk checking in keys told Lyria that he would be working the very next day, so they resolved to return then. Kev and her friends parted when the bell chimed, warning them that afternoon classes would begin soon. Kev reminded them to meet her at the end of the day so they could all go together to meet Eldet at the Outpost.

The sun was bright and leaves rustled in an autumn breeze when Kev left the Scholar's Tower after her last class. She walked toward the street and gazed up the hill, where she could just see the top of the Outpost above the other buildings in the distance. She could just make out the shape of a dragon launching itself from the wall of the Outpost and flying off into the distance.

She waited near the front gate of the Scholar's Tower for Ferra and Lyria to arrive so they could walk together. She was leaning against the wall, keeping an eye on the front doors, when she saw Tanar and his friend emerge. The two boys were laughing at something, and then at a comment from his friend, a black expression took over Tanar's face. Kev moved away from the front gate slowly, toward a group of trees. She did not want Tanar to notice her.

As the boys passed her, she heard Tanar say, "And now we have to *walk* to the fair." His tone was full of bitterness, the word "walk" filled with contempt, and Kev knew she was right to have avoided him. The two boys reached the gate and turned onto the street in the direction of the Onami fair and Kev sighed. She hoped that she wouldn't run into him at the fair today. At least there, the sheer number of people would provide a buffer, even if she did.

"What's got you looking so glum?" came Ferra's voice from behind her. Kev turned to find Ferra and Lyria approaching.

With all the focus on the rats, Lyria's bag, and the other thefts, Kev had not told Ferra of her and her mother's encounter with Tanar's mage driver, or about his attempt to bully her today in class. So she told them now.

Ferra looked increasingly angry while Kev told her tale. "Imagine, having to walk," she said sarcastically. "As if it would kill him. Why don't his parents just hire another cart and driver, if it's so important?"

Lyria giggled. "Unless they're punishing him for the driver getting suspended. Maybe he's the one who told the driver to go so fast."

"I don't know," Kev said. "I didn't want to engage him on the topic. I'm sure anyone could have reported the driver with how badly he was driving. My ma didn't even have time to report anything yesterday. She was stuck at the fair!"

"Oh yeah, good point," Ferra said. "I suppose he wouldn't believe you though."

"He can believe whatever he wants," Kev said. "I just hope we don't run into him at the fair."

They reached the outpost and told the gate attendant they were there to see Eldet. Being so close to the Onami fair, the Outpost had a festive air itself, set up for its own celebration for the autumn harvest. The open yard inside the walls had tables and stands set up with different types of food and drinks, and the gate attendant invited Kev and her friends to try any of the foods for free.

When Eldet found them, they were seated on the grass with handfuls of fried vegetables on sticks, bowls of creamy soup, and cups of apple cider spread out before them. The rats had their own little piles of food scraps that the girls had spared from their own collections.

"I forgot how good the Outpost food is," Kev said, and slid a fried mushroom into her mouth off of the skewer.

"We really need to come visit you more often," Ferra said, grinning.

Eldet rolled his eyes. "Of course you're welcome to visit any time, but don't you worry that you'll be too full for the fair food when you get there?"

"I'll be going again tomorrow," Ferra said with a shrug. "You can't go only one day, if you don't want to miss any of the good stuff."

"That's true," Eldet said. "Maybe I should get some food before we go, now that you say it."

Eldet waited in line for a skewer of fried veggies and chicken, and the girls finished their food quickly so they could walk with him. When Eldet had his food in hand, the group left through the gates of the Outpost and joined the steady stream of people, beasts, and wagons on the road on their way to the Onami fair for the afternoon and evening.

Ferra asked Eldet if his mother had gotten any more information since the day before.

"None that she shared with me," he said. "As usual," he added with a sigh. "Riders aren't allowed to share information from things like this until they're resolved. It makes sense I suppose, but it sure is boring."

"Did you tell her about Lyria's bag being stolen?" Kev asked.

"Sort of, but I don't know if it got through to her. I only

really saw her at lunch today in the great hall, and she seemed pretty distracted."

A shadow passed over their heads, another dragon flying from the Outpost out to the fair grounds.

As they got closer and closer to the fair, the sound of music grew louder, and the smells of fair food drifted their way. Ferra put a hand to her belly and drew in a long breath.

"Mmm," she said. "Maybe you were right about filling up before the fair," she said to Eldet, who laughed in response.

The great road out of town led right through the middle of the fairgrounds, so that even if someone had wanted to skip the fair, they would end up passing right through the thick of it, if they had a cart or wagon that did not allow them to leave the well-traveled road.

The wagons of the Onami caravan stretched out as far as Kev could see, interspersed with signs, banners, and flags advertising all types of different wares that one might be looking for. Every year, the different Onami families that made up the caravan arranged themselves in roughly the same areas. Regular attendees from Mirella and the surrounding farms tended to claim their usual spots as well. And then there were those who wandered throughout the fair carrying their wares on their back or in a basket on their forearm, selling all throughout the fair. Anyone could try their hand at selling something they had harvested or made, if they could catch the notice of fairgoers above the noise from the rest of the sellers.

"My family's wagon is down this way," said Lyria at a smaller dirt footpath that broke off the main road and wound through the rows of wagons and stalls. "Do you mind if we stop by there to say hello?" she asked. Then she lowered her voice. "Just don't mention that we're looking for my case," she said. "They just think I lost it. Like, in a normal way."

Kev nodded. It would be easier that way anyway. Then she didn't have to worry about anyone mentioning her sketches.

Lyria's family's stalls for selling were made up of two wagons side by side in the back, and racks and stands full of clothes spread out before them. Three children, younger than Lyria but probably older than Sayess, Kev thought, sat facing each other in the grass in front of the stall, playing some game with pebbles. When they saw Kev and her group coming toward the stall, they hurriedly jumped up, brushing dust off of their pants and standing up straight.

"It's just me," Lyria said, moving to the head of the group so the children could see her. They visibly relaxed, unstraightening their backs, and the tallest one skipped forward to give Lyria a hug.

"This is my sister Vi," Lyria said, "and my cousins Livvy and Pye. Those are their nicknames." She gestured at the two younger children. They smiled and gave little waves to Kev and her friends, then sat back down and went back to their game in the grass.

Lyria led them through the racks of clothes, which Kev resisted touching. The woven material was very good, and she wondered if her Ma ever traded with Lyria's family for wool or yarn. Lyria's mother was sitting at a counter near the wagons, a pile of knitting in her lap. When she saw Lyria she smiled, stood, and hugged her too.

"There you are!" she said. "And Ferra!" She gave Ferra a hug too, then peered at Kev and Eldet. "And are these your other new friends you've been telling me about?"

"This is Kev and Eldet," Lyria said. "Friends of Ferra's."

Kev smiled and gave a little wave.

"Do you make all of the cloaks here?" Eldet asked. "The fabric is beautiful."

Lyria's ma blushed and swatted a hand at him. "Oh, don't you flatter me," she said. "I make a lot of them, along with my sister. Thank you." She smiled at Eldet and then back at her daughter.

"Well, don't let me keep you, I know you've got better things to do than to hang around the wagon. Oh look, a customer." She moved her knitting from her lap to the table and got up to greet the people who had just entered the stall. Lyria's sister and cousins were already up and greeting them, offering them water, tea, and cookies.

"I'll be right back," Lyria said to her friends and disappeared behind the curtain hanging between the two wagons. Kev could hear her footsteps on the wood floor of the wagon. Lyria returned without her school bag, only carrying a little leather pouch tied on cords around her waist.

"No more packs to lose," Lyria said, patting her pouch with a smile. "Let's go!"

Lyria's sister and cousins waved happily at her and her friends as they left the stall, and Kev almost envied them their pastime of playing games in the grass. But then as she set out with her friends toward her own family's wagons, she felt a thrill of excitement at the thought of solving this mystery.

"So, what exactly is the plan here?" Ferra asked as they made their way down the packed dirt lane crowded with fairgoers.

"I was thinking I would just talk to my ma's cousins, find out what other sellers had things stolen from them, and figure out what to do from there," Kev said.

"Oh. I thought maybe there was more to it than that," Ferra said.

"More to what?" Kev asked. "It's not like I'm a professional seeker. I've never done this before." She hadn't really, not on purpose like this. When she'd searched for Eldet and the weyr-dragon, it had been to clear her own name.

Ferra opened her mouth as if to argue, then stopped and sighed. "You're right."

"Maybe if I buy something from one of the stalls, it'll give me something to draw," Kev said, almost to herself.

Finally they reached the stall that Kev's ma's cousin, Vansal, shared with his wife Kalla. She hadn't yet seen them this fall, so she was greeted with hugs and excited chatter. They informed her that her ma had been there earlier to retrieve her cart and mule, and was now circulating around other parts of the fair doing her trading. Kev introduced her friends to her ma's cousins, who she called uncle and aunt out of habit since childhood. Onami families had so many interconnecting branches, it sometimes became easier to do away with trying to track the exact level of cousin somebody was to another.

Vansal and his wife Kalla were every inch a typical Onami couple, right down to the adornments on their wagon and the wares they sold, including Vansal's herbs and Kalla's spinning and weaving. Vansal was of medium height and lean, though his size belied the strength Kev knew he possessed as one of the helpers to the shepherds in the caravan. He wore his fair hair tied back and a band of plain-woven fabric with little embroideries around his forehead. His tunic was dark brown with reddish orange embroidery at the hems, and his pants tucked into soft leather boots that sported more embroidery, even on the ties that laced the boots closed.

Kalla, full-figured and her fair hair sprinkled with gray, wore a many-layered skirt with beautiful fabrics dyed in a rainbow of colors, covered in the front by a plain apron with several well-used pockets. She wore a light knitted open-fronted sweater over her linen blouse, and her hair was partially pulled back from her face, with small braids with beaded chains woven in them dangling from her temples.

Because of their skill at textiles in all forms and stages of the process, Onami were known to create many new and intricate styles of garments, weavings, and adornments for their bodies, their wagons, and other items. Kalla and Vansal were no exception, Kev thought as she greeted them. Her uncle Vansal's plant dyes were probably responsible for many of the colors in Aunt Kalla's skirts.

It didn't take much for the topic of the disappearance of Vansal's herbs and supplies to come up after Kev had finished introducing her friends. Eldet mentioned that his mother was a dragon rider and that she had been working at the fair the day before, and Vansal eagerly shared about his experience.

"Did they leave you with anything to sell?" Kev asked.

"They only got what I had stored under the table here," Vansal said, gesturing at the work table at the back of his stall. "It was a lot, but it wasn't everything, thankfully." He saw Kev looking at the nearly empty table at the front of the stall. "I've been keeping most things put away in the wagon for now, to be safe. Though it hasn't helped sales much to have it all hidden away."

Kev frowned in sympathy with her uncle. "I hoped I could share some of your autumn spiced tea with my friends," she said. "Do you still have any of that?"

Now Vansal grinned. "We've got plenty in our stores. I'll make up a bag for you." He disappeared into the wagon.

Aunt Kalla had struck up a conversation with Lyria about the adornments in her hair and about the yarn she was spinning. Lyria was looking over Kalla's half of the display table, which was spread out with various types and colors of yarn, thread, and cord. Lyria held several hanks of hemp cord in her hands, all in different jewel-toned colors.

"I lost almost all of my supplies recently, too," Lyria said to Kalla. Since Lyria was part of this Onami caravan outside of the school year, she knew Kalla and Vansal, or at least knew who they were.

"Here at the fair?" Kalla asked, her eyes narrowing with interest.

"No." Lyria shook her head. "In the city, at a cafe near my school. I must have misplaced it." Then she held up her handful of skeins of cord and smiled. "But this will be a good start to replacing my collection of supplies. How much?"

While Kalla wrapped up Lyria's purchase, Vansal came back with a paper bag filled with his spiced tea blend and handed it to Kev.

"A gift," he said when he saw Kev's hands move toward her purse at her waist.

"Thank you, Uncle Vansal," Kev said. When she reached to her satchel to tuck the bag of tea inside, Green Bean and Turnip reminded her of their presence with tickly noses. They sniffed the bag of tea from within their carry pouch.

"Don't you get into this," Kev said. "We'll get you your own treats." When she looked up to see Vansal's surprised stare, she blushed.

"Your ma mentioned your pet rats, but I didn't realize they traveled with you," he said with a laugh.

"Only when they feel like it," Kev said. "Sometimes they just disappear on me. But I think today they're looking forward to me sharing some fair foods."

"Just don't let the foodsellers see them near their stalls," Vansal advised. "They don't like to see rats and mice near their food. And if food starts disappearing like our things have, we don't need anyone blaming your pets!"

"Have any more people lost things since yesterday?" Kev asked. "Since the mage guard and dragon riders started looking into it?"

Vansal shook his head. "Not that I've heard. It was only our little area here that was hit. And word has gone through the whole caravan. If more people had their things stolen, we'd have heard of it by now."

"So only wagons in this section had things stolen?" Kev asked, hoping that she simply sounded curious for curiosity's sake. "That's so strange."

Vansal shrugged. "Maybe not. Whoever it was got whatever he could, then took off when the outcry started, I suspect."

"But where could he go?" Kev wondered, looking up and down the rows of stalls nearby. "How would he escape notice carrying all those things? Who did he steal from?"

Uncle Vansal began to point out different stalls. Besides their proximity to each other, there seemed to be no rhyme or reason to what was stolen. As her mom had relayed last night, there was a painter two stalls down, a leatherworker across the way, an embroidery shop next to that, and a weaver even farther down from the painter on Vansal and Kalla's side of the row. Not only that, but there were also a woodworker, a harper, and scrivener further down the row. Kev tried to remember all of the stalls that Vansal pointed out, and hoped that her friends were paying attention too.

"And everybody lost their tools *and* stock?" Ferra asked, incredulous. "That's horrible!"

Vansal nodded solemnly. "I hope the mages and the dragons can find it before we move on. It's a blow to all our year's work if we can't sell what we gathered and made. Bad enough we can't make all we would have at this fair, let alone all the rest as we go south."

Kalla had come up beside Vansal as he spoke, and Lyria rejoined Kev, Ferra and Eldet with her purchase. Kalla said, "It'll be a miracle if they can find it at all," and shook her head. "It's probably someone trying to make life difficult for us Onami again. One of those who don't want us near their cities, just trying to drive us off."

"You can't know that," Vansal said, but to Kev, he didn't seem too sure.

Kalla took his arm and smiled. "You always think the best of people. I hope you're right, and it's just a common thief who will get caught."

"No doubt the mages can do a lot with their magic," Vansal answered. "And the dragons, too." He nodded his head toward Eldet when he said that.

"At least if they catch the thief after you leave, the dragon riders can bring you your things!" Eldet said.

"I hope so," Vansal said. "But you kids didn't come here to hear about our woes. Go enjoy the rest of the fair! Thanks for the visit, Kev."

If only he knew, Kev thought. She and her friends thanked Vansal and Kalla again, then headed off into the crowd of fairgoers once more.

Evening at the Fair

After they had left Vansal and Kalla's stall, Kev, Ferra, Eldet and Lyria headed down the row to the next stall that her uncle had pointed out, the painter. It was easy to show genuine interest in artists' work that was for sale; it was gorgeous. Kev picked out a small framed picture to buy in case she wanted to use it later as a focus of her drawing.

Kev wanted to make sure she remembered all of the stalls that Vansal had pointed out to her so she could visit them all later, so she found herself a seat on a bench in a little rest spot that had been set up in the middle of the walkway. There, she could write them all down while her friends browsed at the leatherworker's stall across the way.

She set down her satchel and let the rats come out of their carry pouch. She was actually surprised they hadn't let themselves out of their pouch already and given themselves a tour around the fair. Maybe they'd had their fill while they'd been here with Ma yesterday. Kev broke off a few pieces of a pastry she'd saved and handed them to the rats, then got out her notebook. She wrote her list of the vendors that had their items stolen. For some, she even knew what kinds of things had been stolen. Others, Vansal only knew that they'd had things taken, but not detail about what things or how many.

Her list, when it was done, included:

- Leatherworker: a box of small leather pouches with tooled designs on the front, folding case full of leatherworking tools
- Painter: jars of paints and a case full of paint brushes, one small painting
- Embroidery shop: a basket of embroidery thread, needles, scissors, and a large hoop with an unfinished embroidered scene
- Woodworker: items unknown
- Harper: items unknown
- Weaver: table loom taken, possibly other items
- Scrivener: items unknown

She contemplated the list for a moment, then closed her notebook with a sigh. She looked up to find her friends had moved from the leatherworker's stall to the embroiderer's stall next door to it. She was about to get up to join them when she heard a familiar voice that made her stomach sink.

"Ugh, Yeran, what is that? That is disgusting." It was Tanar, and when Kev looked up, he was standing a few feet away and pointing at her. His friend Yeran stood by him with a sneer.

"Come here," Kev said, scooping the rats up into her arms and attempting to stuff them into their pouch. Normally happy to slide into their soft sleeping place, the rats resisted. "Come on," Kev said in as low a voice as she could manage. "It's for your own safety."

Despite her efforts to hide the rats, they remained on her lap, and Tanar and Yeran were now stalking toward her, a disconcerting grin twisting Tanar's features.

"Are those *rats*?" he asked, emphasizing the word rats as if he was spitting out something distasteful that he'd eaten. "And you're touching them? I knew you were a low-born Senemi, but this really is too much." He turned to Yeran. "Pet vermin, can you believe it?"

"I can't believe they allow you into the Scholar's Tower," Yeran said.

"I can't believe they let you into the fair," Tanar answered his friend. Then he laughed. "Do you think they'd let you stay, if I told them? Maybe I should find a fair official." He smiled and made a show of looking up and down the walkway for an official.

Normally, when others had objections to the idea of rats as pets, Kev had a host of answers for them. She would say that the rats kept themselves very clean, that they were no different than having dogs or cats as pets, and that they didn't deserve their reputation. Or she would point out that these rats were bred as pets, evidenced by their different coloring, and that it was different than dealing with wild rats getting into grain stores or roaming the sewers. These were things that she had learned from Tara, the creature seller in the creature courts in the city market, who was the one who had taught her how to care for pet rats.

But she knew that none of those arguments or reasonings would matter with Tanar. He just wanted to make fun of her, not be convinced to change his mind. She put her notebook back into her satchel and cradled the rats so she could stand up.

"If it bothers you that much, I'll just be going then," Kev said in the most neutral tone she could manage. She glanced toward the embroidery shop where her friends still stood. Tanar and Yeran were inconveniently blocking the way between Kev and her friends, and they'd gotten close enough to her that she couldn't easily sidestep her way around them. "Could you please move?" Kev asked.

Tanar just sneered at her. "You'll have to wait. I'm reporting you to the fair officials. They may be dirty Onami, but even they won't want vermin threatening their food stores."

"I don't think so," Kev said, and made to push her way past Tanar in a space between his crossed arms and a shrub next to her bench. As she moved, the rats seemed to melt out of her arms and to the ground, where they promptly took an interest in Tanar's shoes. They each climbed onto one of his feet and began to chew at his laces.

Tanar's smirk quickly turned to an expression of fear, with a flash of anger. Fear seemed to win out, because he began kicking his feet and shouting.

"Get these things off of me! Help!" He flung out his left foot, which Green Bean clung to, and looked horrified when this did not rid him of the rat. In fact, Green Bean began to climb up his leg to get a better grip. Turnip followed her sister's example.

"Yeran, help me! Get them off of me!" Tanar shrieked. He spun in circles, trying to slap at his legs but managing to miss the rats each time. As he spun, he backed away from Kev, and his movements spilled out into the lane of people trying to walk the fair.

Yeran held his hands up in front of him and backed away, apparently afraid the rats would move to him if given the chance.

Kev bit her lip, afraid for her rats' safety and wanting to retrieve them from Tanar, but afraid to get too close to her would-be tormentor's increasingly frantic kicks and swinging arms. She also did her best to hold back a laugh, knowing that would only enrage Tanar further, and would likely have consequences after he had escaped the attentions of Green Bean and Turnip.

Instead Kev took the opportunity to move away from the bench and out of Tanar and Yeran's reach. Once she was well enough away, she called for the rats.

"Green Bean! Turnip! That's enough now! Come!"

"What is going *on*?" asked Ferra, coming up next to Kev from the direction of the embroidery shop.

"That's Tanar," Kev said. "The one from my history of magic class that I was telling you about."

"Huh," said Ferra. "The rats seem to like him."

Kev turned to her friend and found an ironic grin playing on Ferra's lips.

Despite Tanar's flailing, the rats managed to avoid all of his blows, staying just out of reach of his arms while also keeping a grip on his pants so they wouldn't get flung off his legs.

"Come *on*, rats, it's time to go!"

By now Eldet and Lyria had arrived at Kev's side as well.

"Here," Eldet said, handing Kev a paper pouch. "Some of their fish treats should help."

Reluctantly, Kev walked back over to Tanar, who was breathing hard and fighting back tears. Kev almost felt sorry for him. She held out Eldet's little pouch of treats and shook it so that the dried fish biscuits rattled inside the paper.

Immediately, the rats jumped to the ground from Tanar's legs and ran over to Kev, who let them climb up her own legs and into her waiting arms.

Tanar bent forward, still with labored breaths, and stared at Kev with fear and disbelief that quickly clouded over into rage.

"You're a witch," Tanar said, his typical sneer exaggerated into a snarl. "I'll see you punished for that." He jabbed a hand out in the direction of the rats as if he could stab them with his fingers.

"Afraid of a couple little furry animals?" said Ferra. She, Eldet, and Lyria had moved up to join Kev. "What a shame. They actually make wonderful pets."

Slowly recovering from his ordeal, Tanar drew himself back up to his full height and wiped his brow. He glanced back at Yeran, who still kept his distance, looking fearful. Kev wondered if Yeran was more afraid of the rats, or of his friend's resulting anger at being made to look a fool.

"Those things are not normal," Tanar said. "What are they? Demons?"

"Actually," said Eldet, "there's no such thing as demons. The creatures commonly called demons are actually a small species of monkey native to a climate much warmer than ours, and they look nothing like rats."

"I don't think he cares," Ferra said, taking Eldet's arm with one hand, and putting her other arm around Kev's shoulder. She waved over Kev's shoulder at Tanar's momentarily speechless, yet rageful glower. "We'd better be going now. Sorry about the rats, they won't bother you again. Well, I guess I can't guarantee that, but I think you'll be fine if you don't bother Kev!" Her tone was light and cheerful, as if she were saying farewell to a sewing group at the end of a nice chat over tea.

"Ferra," Kev scolded her. "He's not going to take that well. He knows you're mocking him."

"Kev, I don't think he's the type to take anything well, and the rats kind of already ruined it. What happened back there?"

Now that they were walking away from Tanar and Yeran, Kev allowed herself the laugh she had been holding back. Green Bean and Turnip were now perched on her shoulders, hidden under her hair, and Kev petted their heads fondly.

"They were just trying to help me," Kev said. "Tanar and Yeran saw me feeding them on the bench and were making a stink about telling the fair officials that I'd brought 'vermin' into the fair. I tried to leave, but they were blocking my way. So the rats made them unblock my way." Kev shrugged, then started giggling again while she petted the rats. Then she noticed that she was still clutching Eldet's paper packet of fish treats, and rewarded the rats with one each.

"That doesn't even make any sense," said Lyria in her soft voice. "The fair officials wouldn't think twice about rats at the fair. There are all kinds of animals about. Besides, all the grain-keeping wagons have cats."

"Well, let's go to the commons and watch some dancers," Ferra said. "After that I think we need some fun."

They all agreed, and made their way to the large open area at one side of the fair known as the commons. It was here that many of the entertainers among the Onami gathered, taking turns performing music, dances, acrobatics, plays, and any other enter-tainments that could be thought of. The commons was a large enough area that different groups of entertainers could be spread out performing at one time, and it was also surrounded by food carts and stalls offering drinks.

It was getting on in the afternoon, and the bright sun that had beat down on them earlier in the day was lowering in the sky, making for a slightly cooler autumn feel, which Kev was thankful for. It had also been long enough since they'd eaten at the Outpost that she and all of her friends visited the food carts for more food. They came back to gather in a circle near a troupe of dancers performing to the music of a guitar and fiddle player. The friends enjoyed their food while they watched the dancers, and Kev fed the rats little bits of her sweet fried bread and let them take sips of her apple cider when it had cooled down enough for them.

After a few songs, Eldet offered to take up a few coins from each of them to add to the dancers' collection basket. He brought the coins up, then went off in search of more battered and fried potatoes for them all to share. By the time he returned, the dancers had finished and a group of acrobats and jugglers had moved to take their space. Without the music, Kev and her friends chatted over the shared snack.

"I wish I'd had more of a chance to practice with you two," Eldet said to the rats, who had climbed into his lap to share not only his potatoes, but also more of his fish treats. "I'm not exactly sure where to start."

"What are you going to practice with them?" Lyria asked.

"I wanted them to help find things, like your case," Eldet said, scratching his head. "Partly to test out how intelligent they are. My other tests have been too simple for them, I think. But now I'm not really sure what to have them do."

Green Bean stood up from her perch on Eldet's ankle and sniffed the air in the direction of his nose. Eldet leaned down and touched his own nose to the rat's, smiling.

"Well at least we know we can trust them to scare off bullies," Ferra said wryly.

"Oh, I know!" said Lyria suddenly. "What if we hid things for them to find? Kind of like you said, but they could practice with things we hid, before they help to find other things, that we don't know where they are."

Eldet pondered this for a moment. Then he smiled. "I like it," he said. He looked to Kev. "Can we try it now?"

Kev shrugged. "If you can get the rats to do it." She looked down at the rats, who had now curled up in the grass among her crossed legs. "Did you hear that? You have a challenge."

Green Bean yawned in response. Turnip stretched and sat up, sniffing curiously.

"I'll go hide some bracelets," Lyria said, loosening the ties on two of her knotted beadwork bracelets as she stood.

"I'll come with you," Ferra said. "I need to stretch my legs. No peeking!"

The two girls wove their way through the different seated groups until they disappeared into the clusters of people waiting at a group of foodsellers' stalls. Soon they were back, returning from the opposite direction and grinning.

"Your turn!" Lyria said cheerfully as she plopped back down in the grass.

Eldet rose and held out his hands to accept the rats from Kev.

"All right, do you think you can do this?" Eldet said, holding the rats up to his eye level. "I need you to each find one of Lyria's bracelets that are hidden around here."

"I'll come with you," said Kev. "I need a stretch too." She was also curious to see how the rats would do. Not that she was sure she'd see them doing it at all. She half expected them to just disappear as they always did from their cage or her bag, and just reappear with the bracelets.

Eldet carried the rats in his arms until they reached a shady spot under a tree at the outside edge of the commons. Kev agreed with him that it probably wouldn't go over well to just set the rats down in the middle of a crowd of people.

"Here you go," Eldet whispered as he bent down surreptitiously and let the rats crawl down onto the ground. "Bring me those bracelets, okay?"

Kev and Eldet watched as the rats melted away into the crowd, drawing no attention. She hoped they'd draw just as little attention if they went near the food stalls, too.

"I never know how much they understand," Kev said quietly as they waited.

"I think they understand a lot," Eldet answered. "Master Rithorn said that all animals understand more than we think, but mage-raised animals just gain the ability to communicate it with us in a way that *we* understand too. And creatures that are magical by nature, like dragons, are just already born with the ability to communicate with us, in some form or another."

Kev thought that over. She knew that dragons could communicate with people, but only their own riders, except for in very rare cases. They did it with their minds. But she supposed that was only one type of communication. The dragons she'd met had communicated with her in their own ways with gestures and sounds. Just like the rats. It wasn't exactly like speaking, but it still got most of the point across.

Her thoughts were interrupted when Turnip appeared at her feet, seemingly out of nowhere, and stood with her front paws against Kev's leg. She was holding one of Lyria's bracelets.

"Look at you! Good girl!" Kev said as she scooped up Turnip. She held her out to Eldet, who grinned and praised her. He gave Turnip one of the fish biscuit treats.

Green Bean soon appeared at their feet as well, carrying the other bracelet.

"I knew you could do it," said Eldet, bending down to take Green Bean in his hands and dispensing another treat.

The rats quickly finished their treats and looked to Eldet for more. He gave them one more, then said, "You can earn more treats when we do more training." He glanced at the sky. "But I don't think we can do any more today. I need to be getting home."

He was right, the sun was sinking lower on the horizon, and Kev would have to get home as well. They returned to where Ferra and Lyria sat with the news of the rats' success, and the two girls agreed that they needed to be getting home too. They left some coins in the juggler's hats as they left the commons, then walked Lyria back to her family's wagon. Lyria's parents bid the three friends a fond farewell.

"Another time we will have you stay for dinner," Lyria's mother said as they waved, and Ferra, Eldet, and Kev heartily agreed.

The way back to the Outpost road was lined with more wagons and vendor stalls, many of which Kev wished she could stop to look at. They did finally make one concession in order to stop at a glassblower's stall. The bright flame lit up the stall in the dimming evening air, creating a warm scene, and Kev never stopped being fascinated by the way the artists molded the glass with their breath and their movements.

The booth was set up so that the glassblower had a work area with enough space for many people to gather and watch, and then the other half was dedicated to displaying the finished glass pieces, which ranged from tiny, clear jars and vials to elaborate, many-hued vases and swirling sculptures. The larger pieces were on display behind the table where the glassblower's assistants took payments and wrapped up packages.

The glassblower finished the piece she was working on before the crowd and settled it in the annealing oven to allow it to cool in its final form. While the glassblower sipped some water and prepared materials for her next piece, Kev's eyes wandered around the stall toward the finished pieces on display. Her heart caught in her throat when she saw Tanar again, talking with the seller. She touched Ferra and Eldet's arms and nodded in his direction, then did her best to melt out of sight behind them.

Ferra had mentioned wanting to purchase some special jars after they watched the glassblower for a while, so they didn't move on yet.

From a distance, and without the sneering expression Kev was used to seeing on him, Tanar almost looked nice to her. He smiled and seemed to banter with the glass seller, and when he left the stall's table to rejoin the traffic in the walkway, his expression seemed pleasant enough. He looked happy, Kev thought.

When he reached the outside edge of the stall, there were two figures waiting for Tanar, not just the one, Yeran, that Kev was expecting. The second figure was taller, perhaps Tanar's father? But when Tanar said something, the man turned to answer him, and Kev saw that it was her teacher, Mage Carrick Valaso. He smiled and laughed at whatever Tanar had said, and then the three walked off together.

Kev frowned. Why was Tanar at the Onami fair with their teacher? Not just their teacher, but one of the most well-known mages in Mirella, for all he was teaching a history of magic course at the non-magical Scholar's Tower. In class, she'd thought that Tanar was always somewhat rude to Mage Valaso, certainly she did not expect them to be laughing and joking together outside of class.

She tried to shake off the dismayed feeling that scene had caused in her. Tanar and Yeran had probably just run into Mage Valaso here at the fair, and of course Mage Valaso had to be nice to his students when he saw them outside of school. But that laugh... he had looked like he was very comfortable with the two boys.

"Oh good, he's gone," said Ferra, and moved away from the glassblower's workbench toward the stall. Kev shook herself and followed Ferra. There was no use dwelling on it. She disliked Tanar, but she couldn't control how others felt about him, especially including her teacher. She would just file away the mental note that her teacher might be friendly with Tanar, just in case she needed to seek help from a teacher at school in the future. And with that thought, she turned her attention on her friends.

Kev bought a small glass charm shaped like a dragon while Terra got her special jars, and then they finally made their good-byes for the night. Kev clutched the little glass dragon in her hands as she made her way down the hill towards home. They had learned a lot at the fair that day, and she had a lot of work to do.

A Stolen Pencil

On Thursday, the last day of classes before the customary three off days, Kev was finally able to get back into the library to continue her search for books that might contain information about her craftmagic. She had left home early that morning even though she didn't have a class during the first hour of the day. That way, she could make use of that quiet time to browse through the stacks. She also felt fortunate that she did not have History of Magic class today, because she knew she would not be able to face Tanar and Yeran. With a shudder at the thought of what may be in store for her when she next attended class, Kev did her best to put that incident out of her mind for now. Hopefully, over the off days, Tanar's anger would die down and he would leave Kev alone.

Kev did not believe that would be the case, but today she had other things to do.

First, she returned to the history of magic section of the library and began to browse its shelves. The last time she had searched this area, she had been looking for anything about craftmagic, or for titles that had at least seemed to be related to crafts and mages. This time, she wanted to come at the topic from a different direction. Since craftmagic was in danger of being seen as the forbidden bound magic, maybe books about bound magic would help Kev make sense of the possibilities of craftmagic. She hoped she would find something, anything, hidden around the edges of the topic of bound magic.

Having little luck simply browsing through the shelves, Kev went to the card catalog and looked through it to compose a list of likely titles. Overall, not many books about bound magic existed, at least not in this library. Perhaps the Mage Academy had more, but the curators of the libraries at the Scholar's Tower must believe that non-mages had little use for extensive knowledge of a type of magic that was outlawed. They were probably right, but it made it Kev's quest difficult.

Most of the titles Kev found dealt with the identification of bound magic in order to dispose of contaminated magical objects or report the users of such magic to the mage guard. Maybe that type of information would be more helpful than Kev initially thought. After all, if craftmagic really was bound magic, then these books would help her find out. If it wasn't bound magic, then she would know for sure.

But when she went to the shelves to find the books on her list, she was astonished to find that only one was left. The rest had been checked out by others. Were there really that many scholars who were interested in finding and stamping out bound magic? Or maybe it was just one person who was dedicated to the topic.

Kev thought about asking the librarian on duty when the books might be expected back in the library, but the thought of calling attention to her topic of interest made her uncomfortable. For now, she would settle for the one book on her list that was left on the shelves. It was titled simply, "How to Avoid Bound Magic." What exactly did that mean, anyway? The phrase "how to avoid" seemed vague to Kev. She wasn't sure if the book would be for regular people to keep from encountering bound magic in their lives, or maybe for mages to avoid practicing their magic in such a way that it became bound magic. The former seemed to Kev like it would be an exceedingly rare occurrence. If it were the latter, then Kev would expect the book to more likely appear in the Mage Academy libraries instead.

Since it was all she had right now, she settled at her table to begin reading it, resigned to the fact that she wouldn't find any other books on bound magic today. Maybe Eldet would be able to help her find books in the Mage Academy libraries, she thought.

What is bound magic? the book began. Kev sighed. What she didn't need was a basic, surface-level explanation of bound magic. But she would read the first page of the book just in case it held more.

The definition of bound magic is simple: bound magic is magical energy that a mage puts into an object that can work independently of the mage himself. Its opposite, free magic, is magical energy that the mage works and has under his direction and control the whole time he is working with it.

This definition is clear and straightforward, and allows for Arethia to ban bound magic while permitting and promoting free magic as the standard for its numerous licensed mages. Magic, large or small, is worked under the supervision of a trained mage at all times, and never allowed to become a danger to the average Arethian. Bound magic and the objects it might corrupt are discovered and disposed of by the Arethian mage guard so that the average person never need worry about encountering dangerous magic in their everyday lives.

Kev sighed again as she turned the page. It was proving to be as boring as she'd feared. But as she began to read the second page, she straightened in her chair.

But what if magic isn't as simple as that? What if the distinction between bound magic and free magic is blurrier than Arethian mages would have you believe? In fact, there is ample evidence that despite its ban and the appearance of a well-regulated magic system in Arethia, that magical energy is even more present in our cities, towns, farms, and even everyday objects than the mage guard and the rulers of Arethia wants us to know. And much of that rogue magic is the very bound magic that is supposedly forbidden. What's more, the people who are propagating this dangerous, unmonitored magic are often the very people who we are led to believe have no capacity for magic at all.

Unfortunately, the sheer number of these forbidden mages is too much for the mage guard to handle, and it seems they are happy to ignore their existence almost completely. Therefore, it is up to the average person to protect themselves from the secret bound magic that they don't want you to see. This book will offer a guide to recognizing bound magic without the help of a mage, isolating and neutralizing the offending objects, and avoiding these objects when their destruction is not a viable option.

Kev flipped to the front of the book to find the author's name. Cyndia Inbedel, said the title page. Aside from the name, there was no other information about the author.

Although Kev agreed with some of the premises in the first couple pages, the writing style and tone of the book made her uncomfortable. Kev agreed that the distinctions between bound magic and free magic were probably a lot fuzzier than most people, especially the mage guard, liked to admit. She had evidence of that with her rats, and, she thought, probably herself. Otherwise she wouldn't be on this quest for information. But was it as dangerous as this author seemed to believe? How many people thought as she did?

A glance out the window told her that the morning hour was almost over and that she would soon hear the bell warning her that her next class would begin soon. She closed the book and gathered her things, looking wistfully at the sketchbook in her pack. She had hoped to have time for some sketching during this early hour too, but she should have known that looking up the books and reading would take up all of her time. She resolved to take time to sketch some of the things from the fair when she returned home from classes today.

Two classes later, over the lunch hour, Kev went looking for Ferra and Lyria in the art wing library. They had agreed that they would try to find Dinnan again so that Lyria could talk to him as they'd planned to yesterday. Dinnan was at the front desk when Kev entered the art library, sitting at the counter hunched over a book. At least Lyria would have more luck in talking to him today.

Kev found Lyria at the same desk she'd been using a few days ago, but Ferra wasn't with her. Kev knocked lightly on the divider to get Lyria's attention. She was bent over another jewelry work, gripping a small metal ring in pliers and adding it on to the end of a string of beads. She secured the ring and set down her pliers before she lifted her gaze to Kev. She smiled in greeting, but almost immediately a frown returned to her face.

"Is everything okay?" Kev asked. "Where's Ferra?"

"Oh, Ferra had to go home sick. She gets these headaches sometimes, and the only thing that helps them is to lie in the dark."

Kev nodded. Ferra had mentioned her headaches before, though Kev had never witnessed one.

"Did you still want to talk with Dinnan today?" Kev asked.

Lyria grimaced. "Oh, that. I forgot about it, but I guess I'd better. Kev," Lyria leaned out of her work cubicle, scanning the room. Then, in a whisper, she continued, "There's more that happened at the Onami fair. Last night after we left there were more robberies. My family, and a lot of the others, are talking about packing up now and leaving as soon as they can."

"But there's still two weeks left!" Kev said, matching Lyria's whisper. "Do you mind if I sit?" she asked, gesturing at the other chair in Lyria's cubicle. Lyria nodded and Kev took the chair. "What changed that's making them want to leave?"

Lyria looked uncomfortable at that question. She stared at her hands in her lap. "Some of the families think that the thefts are meant to send a message to the Onami. Not just the Onami, but the...the ones who make special works with...well, with their magic." Lyria lifted her eyes to Kev's after she said it.

"You mean like craftmagic?" Kev whispered back. "Like my drawing?"

Lyria nodded. "You can call it that, some do. Others insist it's nothing more than special talent or care that the artisan takes in their work. It's safer that way when we're in towns. Some people call it bound magic, but it's not. It's not the same at all," Lyria said. The words were tumbling out of her mouth, and Kev could see that her hands were shaking.

"But they said the mage guard won't care, that they'll take us in for bound magic if it gets reported that all the thefts were from people who put their talent into their work. They'll come for us instead of the thief, they're saying."

"So you're saying that everyone who got things stolen from them is a craft mage?" Kev asked.

Lyria nodded, biting her lip.

Now Kev wanted to examine the small painting she'd gotten. Would she be able to tell what was magic about it?

"Who else had things stolen from them last night?"

"The glassblower did!" Lyria said a bit too loudly in her excitement, then put a hand to her mouth and looked around the library. "The same one we were watching right at the end. And some others in that area. I can make you a list."

Kev nodded. "Why don't we go talk to Dinnan and get that done. Maybe it won't help at all, but anything is better than nothing at this point."

Kev waited while Lyria organized her jewelry and supplies and set them away in the cupboards at the cubicle, and then they walked together to the front desk where Lyria returned the cubicle Keys to Dinnan.

He took the keys with a smile and a nod and moved to hang them on the peg board on the wall. When he turned around, he looked startled to see Lyria and Kev still standing there.

"Was there something else?" he asked.

"Yes," said Lyria, staring at her hands. Kev hadn't realized she was so shy, even though she knew she was soft spoken. Maybe having Ferra around helped her confidence, so Kev hadn't seen her this shy before. "I just needed to ask you about something, from last weekend."

Dinnan furrowed his brows. "Sure, what is it?"

"You stay in rooms above the Flowermiller Cafe, right?"

"Oh yeah, I've seen you there before, haven't I?" Dinnan said. He ruffled his hair. "Are you looking for a room? I could ask the landlady."

"Oh, no. Um, actually, I lost something at the cafe. Actually, it might have been stolen. And I think I remember that you were there that day, so I wanted to know if you remember if you saw anything odd."

"And what day was this?" Dinnan frowned. "I'm not sure I'll remember anything much past yesterday, but I'll try," he said.

"Saturday. I was sitting at a table by the window doing some beading, and I dropped a bead, and after I bent down to get it, my whole jewelry making case was gone! I know I should be better about watching my things when I'm in public, but I swear it was right by me, and it had all of my tools and supplies, and a lot of my finished jewelry that I was supposed to sell at the fair." Now that she was talking, the words tumbled out of Lyria's mouth like a waterfall.

"You had something stolen while you were at the Flowermiller Cafe?" said a voice behind them.

Lyria jumped and squeaked.

"I'm sorry, I heard a bit of what you said." It was another art scholar who spoke, he was holding one of the large, flat cases that painting and drawing students used to transport their paper art pieces. "I was just wondering, because I had things stolen from me while I was there, too."

"You did?" Lyria asked, glancing at the case.

"Not my portfolio, thankfully," said the boy. "It was my

pencil case and paint set." His face looked pained. "I had some special colors in there, too. Pigments from a trip to Areth that I can't get here. It's going to take some time to replace it all."

"I'm sorry," said Lyria. "It was the same with my tools. It's not quite the same using the ones here. I'm glad for the library of course," she said, glancing apologetically at Dinnan.

Dinnan smiled. "I just work here," he said, raising his hands. "And I'm sorry," he said, addressing Lyria. "I don't think I've seen or heard of anything that can help you. It must have been an opportunistic thief. But I can put in a word with Mistress Flower-miller. I'm sure she and her servers have seen more than I do."

"Thank you," Lyria said to Dinnan, and turned to the art student.

"I'm Lyria, and this is my friend Kev," she said. They shook hands.

"Riskin," said the boy. He looked older than Kev and Lyria, possibly a fourth- or fifth-year scholar, Kev thought. He had smiling brown eyes that peered out from under curly black hair. He was fairly tall and lean.

"Do you mind telling us more about what happened with your paints and pencils?" Kev asked. "We're trying to see if we can track down Lyria's things. If we find where hers are, maybe we'd find yours there too." Kev inwardly winced. She sounded like Ferra now, promising things to people that she wasn't sure she had any chance of delivering on.

"For sure. Should we go talk outside?" said Riskin with a nod toward the library door.

Kev and Lyria nodded and they all walked out together. Kev followed Lyria down the stairs to the courtyard, with Riskin a few steps behind so his portfolio didn't bump into anyone's legs.

Once in the courtyard, the three settled in a nice spot on the grass. Kev decided that if she was going to start taking people's stories, she had better start noting them down, and opened her satchel to retrieve her notebook. She gasped when Green Bean and Turnip popped out of the opening of her satchel before she could reach her hand in. They spilled into her lap and she glared at them.

"I did not give you permission to come with me today," she said. She looked apologetically to Lyria, then Riskin.

Riskin's eyes were wide.

"I'm sorry," Kev said. "They sneak into my pack, and they're really, really good at it."

Riskin made a small noise that maybe was supposed to be a laugh, and looked around the courtyard.

Great, Kev thought. He's probably trying to decide if he should run away.

"They're just pets," Kev added. "They're really nice, if you can ignore the part where they don't stay home when I tell them to." She glared at the rats again. "They won't come near you if you don't want them to. Right, Green Bean and Turnip?" Kev sighed.

"So," said Lyria, "about your paints. Was there anything strange, when they went missing? Like anything weird that happened?"

Riskin took his eyes off the rats and looked at Lyria, eyes wide. "How did you know? There was something. I wasn't sure if they were connected or if it was an odd coincidence."

Kev, with her notebook now successfully removed from her satchel, and the rats reluctantly put back in, scribbled down a note.

"What happened?" she asked. "What happened that was strange?"

"I was drawing with my colored pencils, and when I picked one up, the color had melted clean out of the middle!"

Lyria glanced at Kev. "You mean like it got hot?"

Riskin nodded. "Yes. It didn't feel warm when I picked it up, but it had been heated at some point, because the coloring was all puddled on the table." He shrugged. "I'd heard that colored pencils can melt if they're left in the sun or something, but I've never had it happen to me before."

"You were in a bakery," Kev said. "Maybe it was just too hot in there. Or your pencils were next to your cup of coffee?"

"No," Riskin said, shaking his head. "It was just the *one* pencil. One of the two I was using."

"And then your pencil and paints went missing?" Lyria asked.

"That was awhile later. I got up to get another coffee, and I figured it would be okay to leave my things at the table. I've done it a million times before." He hung his head. "When I got back to the table, all my things were gone."

"Your things?" Kev asked. "I thought it was just your pencils and paints."

"Oh, sorry." Riskin grimaced and scratched his head. "Those were the only things I couldn't replace easily. My sketchbook and papers were taken too, it just wasn't what I was worried about the most." He shrugged.

"You weren't worried about your sketchbook being taken?" Kev asked. She couldn't imagine losing her work like that.

"It was a new one," Riskin said. "Nice book, too. But I didn't lose many drawings."

Kev nodded. That made sense. "Shame about the sketchbook, but glad you didn't lose too much work."

"Exactly," said Riskin. He was looking strangely at Kev.

"What?" she asked.

"You can really keep rats as pets?" he asked.

Kev chuckled. "Do you want to see them again? You can give them a treat."

"Sure," said Riskin with a smile. "Sorry about before. I just wasn't expecting to see rats pop out of someone's school bag today."

"Me either," Kev said wryly.

A Visit to the Outpost

"This doesn't make any sense!" growled Lyria as she and Kev left the Scholar's Tower. They'd talked with Riskin the rest of their lunch hour, and when they had to return to classes, Kev had agreed to meet Lyria and walk with her to the Outpost. Lyria was staying at her family wagon in the caravan as long as the Onami fair was in town, and would later take up her boarding room at the Landir Lodging Houses during the school year after the caravan left for the winter. Kev had told her parents that she would be right home after her classes today, but she would send a note with one of the messenger mages at the Outpost if they stayed long talking to Eldet.

"What doesn't make sense?" Kev asked.

"Riskin, and the Flowermiller Cafe." Her forehead scrunched up as she thought. "If someone is targeting Onami because of our craftmagic, then why did Riskin get his things stolen? He's not Onami."

"He must have craftmagic then," said Kev. "If that's the common factor. Are we sure it's not just a coincidence, though? That all of the Onami who were stolen from have craftmagic?"

"I don't know!" Lyria blurted. "That's what's so frustrating! Until he came along, I thought I mostly understood what was going on. The explanation made sense, at least. Not everybody likes the Onami." The last part, she said quietly.

"We don't really know why any of these things have been stolen," Kev said, thinking aloud. "Because several of the Onami vendors were stolen from right after your case was stolen, we assumed they were linked. And maybe they are," Kev said, forestalling a protest from Lyria, who had her mouth open, ready to retort. "But we don't know for sure. And even if they are all the same person, or people, how do we know that it's because they're Onami, and not just because the fair was a convenient place to steal from? And the cafe? Maybe it's just someone who wants to sell the crafts somewhere else." Kev shrugged.

"What about the strangeness with my beads, and Riskin's pencil?" Lyria asked.

"I don't even know where to start with that," Kev admitted. "We might have to set that aside for now."

"If someone were stealing things just to sell, why are they taking tools and supplies, too? Why not just the finished work?"

"You said they were your best tools?" Kev asked.

Lyria pursed her lips, then nodded. "Yes, some were custom made."

"Tools and supplies have value at the secondhand markets," Kev said thoughtfully. "Or maybe it was just easier for them to grab the case and run before you noticed."

Lyria groaned. "So you think it could just be random?"

"I don't know," Kev said. There was something niggling at the back of her mind that she hadn't quite uncovered yet.

"That makes it even worse!"

Kev stopped walking. "What?" How could a random thief be worse than somebody targeting the Onami?

"If my things were stolen for no good reason, then we have nothing to go on besides your drawing. And I'm so thankful for that, really I am," Lyria said with a weak smile at Kev, "but now we know that Dinnan didn't see anything, he just lives above the Flowermiller Cafe, so we're out of clues, and I'll never get my supplies back!" She clenched her fists, then crossed her arms, hugging herself. Kev thought she saw tears welling up in her eyes.

Kev took Lyria's arm and led her out of the main traffic of the road. They were getting close to the Outpost now, but the hill got steeper as it got closer, and they could use a rest anyway. They sat on a bench between two shops while Lyria caught her breath. Kev found a clean kerchief in an outside pocket of her pack and handed it to Lyria.

"Do you mind telling me about your craftmagic?" Kev asked softly. "I never knew it existed until a few months ago, and then I only found out about mine because I was using it by mistake." She laughed. "That's probably why my picture isn't doing any good."

"But Ferra told me about the other pictures you drew, that helped you find the weyrdragon, and Eldet," Lyria said. "She seemed to think you were very good at it."

Kev laughed again. "I've only known Ferra for a few months too. I'm glad she has such confidence in my abilities. I wish I did. I...actually don't really know where to start trying to figure it all out. I've been trying to find books and things, but I haven't had lots of luck."

Lyria nodded. "It's dangerous to put it into writing, so I'm not surprised."

Kev thought about mentioning the craftmagic book that her teacher at her old school, Mage Maren, had given her, but she decided to keep that to herself for now.

"You're Senemi, right?" Lyria asked.

Kev nodded.

"Then you know how it is for Onami. People don't trust us. They think we're beneath them. Especially mages." She made a face.

"Some mages think everybody's beneath them," Kev said with a laugh. Then she scowled, thinking of Tanar and his mage driver. "And people who can afford to hire mages."

"Well, anyway. Maybe Onami can't be true mages, but we all

have our crafts and our talents. Mine is working with jewelry, all kinds. It's not really that different than making jewelry without magic, it's just that, sometimes when I'm working, I get really focused on the piece I'm making, and I kind of lose track of everything around me, and some of that goes into my work. And sometimes I can try to move it in a certain direction, or think about a certain thing, like luck or happiness, and those things will become part of the pieces I make. But I don't exactly control it on purpose. It's just part of my making. Do you understand?"

"I think so," Kev said, thinking back to times she'd drawn things or people that were true and real without having ever seen them before. She couldn't really say if she had been trying hard to draw them on purpose. She thought she recognized the state of mind that Lyria had described.

"You said you had a protection on your jewelry making case," Kev said absently as her mind wandered. "Was that craftmagic? Did you put the protection on it?"

"Partly," Lyria said. "My ma's friend wove the fabric, and she weaves fabric that keeps things safe, protected. It's not perfect, but it helps. Like it's charmed. And then my ma sewed it, and she kept protection in her mind too. Then I made the clasps that held it shut. So it's not like what I think of as bound magic. There's not separate magic in the bag, they're not separate things at all. But there is magic in it, it's just that the craft and the magic, and the skills I use to make it, are all the same thing." She winced and glanced at Kev. "I don't know if that makes sense how I said it, but it's hard to put into words."

"I think I understand," Kev said, staring out past her feet at the road, not really seeing. They sat quietly for a bit. "Did you need training in it?" Kev asked after a while.

Lyria shook her head. "Not like what you're thinking," she said. "Besides my training in beadwork. The better I got at that, the more I could really use the craftmagic with it. I guess it's like anything, you have to practice it."

With a sigh, Lyria stood from their bench. "We'd better get going if we want to catch Eldet."

At the Outpost, the two girls were directed to find Eldet in the stables. The stables were named just like the ones meant for horses, but at the Outpost, the stables housed dragons. Kev had never been to the stables before, and although she had recently grown more comfortable around dragons than she used to be, she still wasn't used to being around them. Especially not this many all close together. She shuddered as they passed through the large open doors at the front of the stable.

She was pleasantly surprised to find the stable fairly empty. Here and there, a dragon rested in a stall, but most were empty. The dragons seemed to stay in the stalls of their own accord, because the stalls didn't have gates in the front of them, just dividing walls between each one. They passed a dragon laying curled up at rest and another eating from a trough of raw meat, and yet another rubbing up against stiff bristled brushes mounted on the wall. The ceilings of the stable were high enough to accommodate perches built into the walls and spanning across the rafters, but no dragons currently lurked in the shadows above.

Kev realized she had no idea how many dragons were housed in the Mirellan Outpost. Never having been a big fan of dragons, she hadn't thought on the subject much before. Today, she was happy to see fewer dragons rather than more.

They found Eldet in a large open stall with an orange dragon. The dragon and Eldet were soaking wet, and Eldet scrubbed a soapy brush along the dragon's neck. Kev noticed the dragon's half-lidded eyes blink slowly as Eldet scrubbed, and—was it purring?

Eldet looked up and smiled when he saw Kev and Lyria approaching. They stopped well back from the dragon, avoiding a puddle of soapy water that ran from the stall to a drain in the floor in the middle of the aisle. Eldet put his brush down and turned the knob on a spigot on the wall behind him. Water showered down from a fixture above the dragon, rinsing the soap away. The dragon leaned from side to side to let the water reach all parts of it, and twisted its neck back so that the water spilled on its head, too.

A few droplets splashed onto Kev from where she stood, and she was surprised to find that the water was warm.

"It's heated?" she said, looking around for a furnace, or signs of one.

"Mages," Eldet said, noting her eyes searching. "There are several on duty here all the time. Not counting any riders that are mages too." Eldet's voice was subdued and his shoulders drooped. He looked like he could use a warm shower himself.

"Are you okay?" Kev asked.

Eldet looked at her questioningly, then laughed. "Just tired. I've been helping with the dragon handlers all day. Almost all the riders have been called out on shifts for the fair. They're patrolling it now, and keeping an eye on everyone who's coming and going."

"Did you talk to your ma about Lyria's tool case last night?" Kev asked.

"A little bit," Eldet said. "She was pretty distracted. She thought it was interesting, especially the bit about the bead, but she didn't seem to think it was linked to the thefts at the fair. She said the mage guard have some leads in the city."

Kev and Lyria exchanged looks.

"About that," Kev said. "We found someone else with a theft connected to the Flowermiller Cafe."

Eldet's eyebrows rose. "Oh?" He walked over to the spigot and turned off the water. The dragon shook itself off, splattering droplets all over Eldet, and some reached Kev and Lyria's feet. They stepped backwards in case the dragon shook again.

Shaking his head, Eldet moved out of the stall and beckoned for the dragon to follow him. Kev backed up even further, trying to avoid the swishing wings and tail in the aisle between the stalls.

"I need to bring Syoni to her stall to dry. Can you walk along with me?" Eldet asked.

Kev was surprised to find that the dragon followed him with

only a gesture; it wore no harness or reins like a horse or a mule would. But then, it made sense when she thought about it. Dragons were far more intelligent than horses, and they worked with their human riders almost as equals. They didn't need a harness for them to know what handlers wanted them to do, even if the handlers couldn't speak to them mind to mind like their own riders could.

After depositing Syoni in a nice dry, straw-lined stall, Eldet joined Kev and Lyria in the aisle. He looked down at himself and grimaced.

"I think I need to get dry too. You can come to our rooms and tell me about it on the way. Do you want to stay for dinner?" he asked.

"I'll need to send a message to my parents if we do," Kev said.

Eldet nodded. "I'll show you where the messenger mage's window is."

The stables were connected to the main building of the Outpost by a long, wide hallway with large windows on each side that were now open to the mild fall air. They entered into a side alcove connected to the great hall in the Outpost. The great hall was a big open room with tables spread throughout the main floor for the humans, and perches, cubbies, and rafters made especially for the dragons. At the back end of the great hall, a set of stairs climbed up to another floor that was open to the main floor. Kev knew from past visits that the living quarters for the riders, their families, and other Outpost staff lay behind the several doors and hallways on that second floor.

Eldet led them through the great hall to a small window near those back stairs and introduced her to the mage who sat at a desk behind the window to take messages. Kev wrote down her message to her parents, and the mage took it, promising to deliver it. The message would be sent to a mage at a message post in the city near Kev's home, and then a runner would bring it to her home. After that, Eldet brought them up the stairs and down a hallway to his family's rooms.

Eldet, his sister Tanis, and their mother shared an apartment. The main room, which they entered now, contained a hearth and a sitting area near the front, as well as a large open balcony, presumably for the dragon to be able to visit the apartment when needed. To the right of the balcony were two doors and then a set of stairs.

"You can wait here, I'll be right back," Eldet said, then trotted up the stairs. He returned about fifteen minutes later in dry clothes, his hair still wet, but smelling of soap now instead of the dragon stalls.

"Thanks for waiting," Eldet said, joining them in the sitting room. He plopped down in a chair across from the couch that Kev and Lyria had chosen to sit on and crossed his legs beneath him. "Did you bring the rats?" he asked hopefully, looking at Kev.

"I'm pretty sure I've still got them," said Kev, unfastening the buckle on her satchel. "That doesn't always mean anything with them though." She peeked inside and saw the rats there, still sleeping after their long walk up the hill. They uncurled and sleepily sniffed the air, then perked up when they realized they were no longer at school. Kev held the satchel out to Eldet, who reached inside and scooped out the still-sleepy rats.

While Eldet played with the rats and fed them treats, Kev and Lyria recounted their talk with Dinnan in the art wing library and then their subsequent talk with Riskin.

"And it happened just within the last week?" Eldet asked.

The girls nodded.

"Then the thieves aren't targeting Onami like they think," he said. "It's something else."

"Craftmagic," Kev said. "It seems like everyone uses craft-magic in the making of their wares, and it's the wares and the tools that are being stolen."

Eldet frowned and looked thoughtful as he stroked between Green Bean's ears. Green Bean's eyes boggled and she bruxed her teeth. Turnip had disappeared into the apartment somewhere.

Kev hoped that Eldet's ma and sister wouldn't mind. Eldet looked up at Lyria.

"You've got craftmagic, in your jewelry?" he asked softly.

Lyria nodded, holding his gaze. Kev saw that she was worried about telling yet another person about it. She hoped Lyria knew she could trust Eldet even though he was a mage.

"Don't worry," Eldet said, obviously thinking along the same lines as Kev. "Most of the mages at the academy don't even believe it exists, and the ones that do believe it exists think it's so inconsequential that they wouldn't even bat an eye to hear someone mention it. Well, maybe they'd roll their eyes." Then he winced. "Sorry, I'm not trying to insult it. I'd like to study it more sometime, actually. But not under most of my teachers. I just meant I won't tell anybody."

Lyria was laughing now at Eldet's bumbling attempt to reassure her. Ironically, it seemed to have actually worked.

"Well, Ma hasn't been able to tell me much about what the riders and the mage guard have found out." He sighed. "She says she's not allowed to."

"That makes sense," Lyria said.

"I know, but I wish it didn't!" said Eldet. Then he looked up from the rats in his lap and grinned at Kev and Lyria. "But I think I have an idea. Can you meet me at the Flowermiller Cafe tomorrow night?"

Kev and Lyria exchanged glances.

"The cafe is closed in the evenings," Kev said.

Eldet smiled even wider. "Exactly."

"I'm not sure I like this," said Kev.

"Don't forget to bring the rats."

Rats in the Cafe

Friday morning dawned cool and rainy. Though Kev loved autumn, she tended to forget that for as many days of sun-drenched breezes and fiery trees, there were often as many rainy, cold, and overcast days sprinkled in among them too. Her Ma decided not to go to the Onami fair that day, even though the weekends were usually its busiest days. This weekend would be the exception if the weather stayed wet and dreary. She hoped that the rainy weather would at least put a hold on any more trouble at the fair.

Kev spent the morning by the hearth doing her readings for her classes and sipping from a mug of hot cider that she periodically filled from the pot that her family kept simmering on the stove. Her two youngest siblings, Kadan and Sayess, had gone with their da to the docks so they could work off some of their energy outside. They'd bustled out the door in their rain coats and boots, ready to pick up rocks along the beach between docks, Kev was sure. It had always been one of her favorite things to do on rainy days too. Maybe she would join them tomorrow if they went again, after she had finished her schoolwork.

That left Kev, her other younger brother Jaen, and Ma at home, so the house was quiet. Jaen had schoolwork to do as well, and he shared the space around the hearth with Kev and Ma. It was a nice cozy morning, Kev thought, but she wished she could stop worrying about Eldet's plans for this evening. She hoped it wouldn't still be raining. Eldet had assured her that he did not plan for anything that could get them into trouble, but she wasn't sure she believed that. Even if he didn't plan it, she worried that it might turn out troublesome anyway.

Her mind kept wandering, too, to her conversation with Lyria about craftmagic yesterday. Lyria had said that craftmagic didn't take any formal training in magic, at least Lyria's hadn't. She had said she practiced and studied her jewelry craft, and that the magic came in those moments when she was truly immersed in her craft.

Maybe Kev needed to try drawing again.

Kev always did her best drawing when she could be alone and quiet in her room. After she finished enough school reading for the morning, she excused herself from the living area and went up to her room. She lit the brazier in her room to fight off the chill in the air and allow her hands to stay warm as she drew.

Turnip and Green Bean joined her on the bed as she took out her drawing supplies and arranged them in her lap and around her. The rats tried to take some of her pencils, but she took them back and gave them some small wood toys of their own to play with. They spent time moving all of the wooden shapes under her blankets, where they made a nest.

In addition to her pencils and sketchbook, Kev also took out the various items she'd bought at the fair, including the blown-glass pendant and her little painting, which she propped up in her windowsill. She also brought out Lyria's bracelet. In place of Riskin's supplies, she would use her own colored pencils to envision his lost pencils and supplies.

When she had her sketchbook propped on her lap and a freshly sharpened pencil in her hand, she paused and closed her eyes. She drew in a breath, breathed out, and thought about all she knew about Lyria's stolen jewelry supplies and all the other people who had had things stolen from them. She thought about the cafe and Dinnan, meeting Riskin in the art library, and watching the dancing flames of the glassblower at the fair just before she must have had her own things taken.

When she began to draw, she still wasn't quite sure what she was going to draw. She started with a few horizontal lines, letting herself feel the texture of her pencil on the paper. Then she started building upon those lines, sketching lightly, until she had the outlines of an Onami market stall. The awning over the stall took shape, the selling table up front, then the silhouette of the wagon behind everything else. And then—the flames of the glassblower's forge began to dance in the front display. Ah, the glassblower it would be, then. Kev touched the pendant she now wore at her neck.

The scene began to take shape under her pencil, growing and filling out as she drew. The glassblower stood behind her forge with her tongs and pipes, pulling and wrapping the glass, which barely seemed like glass to Kev at all in this state, until it melded into the desired shape. The scene was frozen like that, before the glassblower placed it in the other oven to cool and hold its shape.

Once the glassblower was captured in motion in the drawing, Kev moved to filling in the surrounding details. She added the table full of supplies behind the glassblower, the selling table to the left side, the curtains separating the selling stall from their wagon and their living space. Then came the people, starting as mere ghosts of an outline at their places in the scene, then becoming real as more details came to Kev and she filled them in.

The sketch work was not quite finished when her ma called up to her for something, and Kev came out of her daze. She blinked at her image so far, not sure that it had told her anything yet, or whether it ever would. But what had taken shape under her hand was clearly not going to be finished in one sitting, or even a day, so Kev decided to put it away for now. She would make time to return to it tomorrow. She felt pleased with herself, having allowed herself time and space to work on her art, and had the feeling that something would come of it for sure.

Luckily, the rain had reduced to an occasional drizzle by dinner time, so when Kev prepared to leave to meet Eldet at the Flowermiller Cafe, she didn't need to think up much of an excuse to tell her family where she was going.

"I'm going for a walk to the Tower library. I need to get out and stretch my legs while it's not pouring," Kev said as she gathered her satchel, rats included, and put on her raincoat.

It was getting dark outside earlier each day, so Kev brought a small oil lantern with her just in case she would end up walking home in the dark. She tried to reassure herself that she would not need it inside the cafe, because they were definitely not going to be breaking into the cafe.

But if they weren't breaking into the cafe, what else did Eldet have planned? She frowned to herself and plodded on, listening to the tiny patter of drizzle on her hood.

The square outside the Flowermiller Cafe was mostly empty of people, just like the rest of the streets, but many of the shops and eating houses were still open and boasted warm, glowing windows that looked inviting against the overcast grayness outside. Even though her belly was still full with warm stew she had just eaten at home, the smell of cooking meat and frying dishes that wafted into the square made Kev wish she was going to one of those eating houses instead of meeting Eldet and Lyria outside an empty bakery that was closed for the day.

Kev passed through a small side walkway between two buildings in the corner of the square, which brought her to the alley behind the shops and cafe. The alley was dimly lit from the shops that were still open, and the Flowermiller Cafe itself had a few windows glowing on the top floors where there were rooms for boarders like Dinnan. When Kev reached the back of the cafe, she found Eldet there, leaning against the wall across the alley from it. He was protected from the rain by a little awning that stretched out over the back door of the other establishment.

Eldet straightened and waved at Kev's approach. Before they

finished greeting each other, Lyria came trotting down the other side of the alley. Eldet eyed Kev's pack.

"Did you bring them?" he asked.

"Of course I did," Kev said, and opened the flap of her satchel. "Green Bean, Turnip," she said softly. "Would you like to have some fun?"

She offered them her hand, and one by one they climbed into her palm and allowed her to lift them out of the satchel. She handed the rats to Eldet, who smiled and put them on his shoulder. Then he turned to Lyria.

"And you brought your things?"

Lyria nodded and pulled some cloth pouches out of her own satchel. From one, she dumped out a pair of beaded bracelets. From the other, she spilled out a small pile of glass and stone beads, along with a few metal findings.

Eldet had a delighted gleam in his eye as he took Lyria's jewelry and beads and held them up to the rats on his shoulders.

"Now, Green Bean and Turnip, we need your help," he said as the rats leaned forward to sniff at the items in his palms. "These are some samples of Lyria's jewelry that she's made, and her supplies. I need you to take a good look at them and pay attention to their magic."

The rats continued to sniff, their noses pressing into the jewelry. Turnip opened her mouth and moved to take one of the bracelets.

"No no, Turnip!" Eldet said cheerfully. "You can't have these until we're done."

"Until we're done?" Lyria squeaked.

"Oh, I thought we could let the rats have them if they wanted. They like little baubles," Eldet said, looking a little abashed. "Is that okay? If they want them, that is."

Lyria looked to Kev, who shrugged. "I didn't know my rats were going to get paid for this. Besides treats, I mean. Maybe you can make them rat-sized bracelets, er, maybe collars, or would you call them...rat necklaces?" Kev offered, stifling a laugh. "That way you can keep those to sell at the fair."

"That's fine," Lyria said. "Especially if we find my supplies case. Then I'll have plenty."

"All right then," said Eldet. "Now that you know what you're looking for, I need you to go into this cafe," he pointed at the back door of the Flowermiller Cafe, "and see if you can find anything—absolutely anything—that smells like or has the same magical tracing as Lyria's jewelry. All right?"

Eldet returned the bracelets and beads to Lyria, who put them safely back in their pouches. Then he crouched low to the ground and extended his arms so they were like ramps. The rats ran easily down his arms to the cobblestone floor of the alley and crossed to the back door of the cafe. They stood on their hind legs and turned to look at Kev.

"How are they supposed to get in?" Kev whispered.

"Isn't that one of their talents?" Eldet whispered back. "Turning up just about anywhere?"

Kev nodded reluctantly. "It's just, I never actually see them do it," she said, watching the rats still standing at the back door, turned to stare back at her. After a moment, they seemed to decide that Kev wasn't going to be any help to them, and scurried along the edge of the building, Green Bean in the lead. The fuzzy gray and white rat led her sister Turnip to a grate at the bottom of a downspout from the roof of the cafe. The two rats squeezed between the bars of the grate and disappeared.

"That doesn't seem like it leads into the cafe," Lyria said.

"Maybe they just need privacy to do their magic," Eldet said with amusement in his voice.

"Or maybe they're looking for a way in from the roof," Kev said. "I'm sure the back door is pretty well locked up."

"So, what do *we* do now?" Lyria asked. She looked up and down the alley. "Isn't it going to look a bit strange for us to just be waiting around in the alley?"

Eldet's mouth dropped open. "Um, I hadn't really thought

about that." He gazed at the back of the Flowermiller Cafe, thinking. "We should probably wait here as long as we can, so the rats can find us when they're done."

Kev thought about pointing out that the rats could usually find her when they wanted to, seemingly no matter where she was, but she didn't like the thought of leaving them. She stared at the back door of the cafe, imagining what the rats might be up to inside. What was she thinking? She'd just sent rats into a bakery and cafe, a place they would clearly be unwelcome if anybody were to see them. She closed her eyes and breathed deeply. The rats would be fine. They had an uncanny ability to hide themselves, she reminded herself.

A loud crash sounded from inside the building, and then a shout.

Kev grabbed Eldet's arm. "What do we do?"

He looked at Kev with wide eyes. "Just stay calm for now. We don't know it's them for sure."

Lights flickered in the windows above the cafe as figures passed in front of them, making shadows. There was more shouting, with two voices that sounded like a man and a woman's. Then a light dimmed in one window and appeared in another. Then that light went out, and the cafe went quiet.

"Maybe we should wait somewhere else, just in case," Eldet said.

Before anyone could move, the back door of the cafe slammed open, and a girl wearing an expression of fury burst through it. She stopped when she saw the three friends standing across the alley from her, then shrugged.

She leaned into the cafe and yelled up the stairs inside, "Don't expect me to ever help you with anything like that again!"

She slammed the door behind her and stomped away down the alley, swinging a lantern beside her and muttering to herself.

"We'd better go," Kev said, looping her arms through Eldet and Lyria's elbows and beginning to walk in the opposite direction from the one the girl had gone. Moments later, the door swung open again, and the man's voice shouted after the girl. Kev snuck a peek over her shoulder as they tried to walk casually away. She couldn't quite get a good look at the man since his back was to them as he called out to the girl.

They came to a gap between buildings and ducked inside it until they heard the door close again. After a few minutes of silence, Kev leaned slightly out the gap to check on the area they'd just left. The alley outside the Flowermiller Cafe was quiet again.

"Maybe we should go back around out to the square," Lyria said in a small voice. "Just in case people are looking out into the alley now, with all that commotion."

"I'm worried that the rats had something to do with that commotion," Kev said, still staring at the back door. She glanced back at Eldet, who wore a perturbed expression.

"I hope they would be smart enough to stay out of it," he said, but he sounded worried, too. "Maybe we should try to go in and check on them," he said.

"Eldet!" hissed Kev. "You said we weren't breaking in!"

"How would we even do that?" Lyria asked. To Kev's surprise, the timid girl sounded almost more interested in the answer to the question, rather than afraid of it.

"Yeah, how would we do that?" Kev said, turning away from the alley now and fully facing Eldet.

Eldet smiled and waved his fingers as a brief glow emanated from them. "I learned a few tricks from the mages who kidnapped me last spring. They made me look for the weyrdragon in lots of places that were locked up."

Cautiously, they moved out of the gap they were hidden in and walked back toward the cafe. They paused at Eldet's signal when they were a few yards away.

"Give me a moment," he said. He closed his eyes and seemed to be concentrating. When he opened them again, they had a faraway look that he directed toward the cafe. His hands moved slightly but not deliberately at his side as he stared at the cafe, and he grimaced a few times and moved his lips as if talking to himself.

"Okay," he said, closing his eyes again. When he opened them, the faraway look was gone. "We can go in now."

They padded softly along the alley toward the back door.

"This Dinnan from the Scholar's Tower who boards here, is he a mage?" Eldet whispered as they tiptoed along.

"I don't know," said Lyria. "I don't think a mage would work at the art library in the Scholar's Tower."

"Well, one of the tenants here right now is a mage," Eldet said. "There were a few warning spells on the locks that I had to shift. Whoever he is won't notice us go in now."

"Warning spells on the locks? Wouldn't that be bound magic?" Kev asked.

Eldet shook his head. "Not if the mage maintains it constantly. It's low enough energy that he could do it in the background if he's got the right kind of talent."

"Could the mage living here be the one who magicked my things and stole them?" Lyria whispered.

Eldet raised an eyebrow at her idea, but then put a hand to his lips. They were now at the door. Slowly, he turned the knob and eased the door open. The entryway was completely dark now that the man from before had left it. Eldet called up a soft light in his palms so they could see where they were going. To the right were the stairs that the shouting girl and the man had descended. Ahead, double swinging doors led to the bakery and cafe.

They pushed through the doors and held them as they swung shut again so they wouldn't make any noise. The inside of the cafe was dark except for the light in Eldet's palm. Tables, chairs, and other furniture hunched in the shadows like waiting monsters.

"What do we do now?" asked Lyria.

"Um, try to find the rats," Eldet said, his voice flat. "Let's try to call them."

He held his hand out before him, and the ball of glowing light in it brightened, making the objects in the room more defined and less shadowy.

Kev glanced toward the front of the cafe where the large

windows always stood open during the day. Now, the wooden shutters were closed over the window and locked, and the outdoor tables and chairs were piled inside on and around the indoor tables.

"Tch tch," said Kev as loudly as she dared, then called, "Green Bean, Turnip! Can you come to us now?"

"I'll look in the pantry," Lyria said and disappeared through a door behind the baking counters. A few seconds later, she returned to the door. "Can I get some light in here?"

At a gesture from Eldet, a new globe of soft yellow light appeared bobbing in the air above Lyria's head. She smiled and returned to the pantry, the light following along behind her.

Kev and Eldet moved about the open cafe space, peering under chairs and tables and examining the contents of storage cupboards along the back wall. They completed a full circuit of the room and found no sign of the rats, and met again by the back door that led to the stairs and the alley.

"What if they're upstairs?" Kev asked. "We don't know how many people might be up there. And it's not even that late. What if somebody leaves for supper?"

Eldet grimaced and peered up at the ceiling. "Maybe we should go back outside. There are a lot of lodging rooms here."

A thump sounded on the stairs and he froze. Kev widened her eyes and looked at Eldet questioningly.

"The pantry," Eldet whispered, and closed his palm, extinguishing his light. He took Kev's hand and guided her to the pantry door, where the light he'd given Lyria still glowed around the edges of the door. When they reached the door, that light dimmed too, leaving just enough light so they wouldn't trip over anything. Kev and Eldet snuck through the door as yet another thump came from the stairway.

"What is it?" asked Lyria, coming over to them and huddling beside them. Now that they were all together, Eldet extinguished the other light. They sat in silence.

Another thump, then another, as if something were dragging

down the stairs. Then there was a dragging sound, like something sliding along the polished wood floor.

Kev would have exchanged glances with Eldet if she could see him, but as it was, she just had to sit silently in the dark. The sounds didn't sound like human footsteps. But what could it be? The rats didn't make that much noise when they walked either.

The sliding sound got closer and closer, and then the pantry door creaked open, then softly bumped shut again.

Kev bit her lip, waiting for a light, or for someone to speak.

The sound started up again, and finally Eldet set another light, this time low to the ground and placed somewhat farther away from himself, Kev, and Lyria.

The light revealed Turnip and Green Bean, awkwardly pulling something large and rectangular along behind them. When Eldet brightened his mage light, Kev saw that the object was a leather-bound book.

"Green Bean! Turnip!" Eldet exclaimed in a whisper. "You did it!" He stood and went over to them to scoop them up, along with the book. He handed the book to Kev and cuddled the rats close to him. "Yes, yes; I've got your treats," he said.

Kev rolled her eyes at the rats' enthusiasm for Eldet's fish treats, and maybe a little bit at their enthusiasm for her friend. They were supposed to be her pets, after all. She crouched and brought the cover of the book into the small light that Eldet had made near the floor.

"On the History of Free Magic and Bound Magic," it was titled. She narrowed her eyes at the book. Did the title sound familiar? Could it be one of the books that she had been looking for in the library the day before? She tucked it into her satchel and touched Eldet's elbow.

"We'd better go," she whispered.

Just as she said it, footsteps creaked in the hall above them, and all three of the friends gasped and went silent. Eldet extinguished his light.

As silently as they could, they moved toward the door of the pantry with Kev in the lead. When she reached the pantry door, she pulled it open just a crack. The entryway and landing beyond was still dark; the footsteps still confined to the floor above them. Kev pulled the door open wider and they filed out.

Voices above joined the sound of the footsteps. There were at least two other people upstairs.

"We need to go!" Lyria's voice was barely contained in a whisper, as if she were about to shriek.

Kev darted from the pantry door to the back door of the cafe and pulled it open. At just that moment, the door at the top of the stairs opened. The voices got louder, and the stairs creaked under the weight of more footsteps.

Kev ran out the door and hoped Eldet and Lyria were close behind. She held her satchel to her side as she ran so it wouldn't bounce about, and made her way to the dark little area between buildings where they had hidden before. Eldet and Lyria tumbled in behind her and they all stopped, breathing hard.

"Hello? Is someone out there?" called a young woman's voice from the direction of the cafe. Then, more quietly, she said "I could have sworn I heard someone at our door."

"It was probably just the wind," said a male voice. "Nasty day it's been, with all the rain. Let's go get dinner."

Their footsteps faded and the voices along with them. When it had been quiet for a long while, Eldet created another light and the three emerged from their hiding place.

"Let's get out into the square before we run into anyone else," Lyria said unhappily. Then, "Oh wonderful, it's begun to rain again."

When they got to the square, they stopped in the shelter of the awning doorway of an eating and drinking house, letting the music drifting out from inside mask their voices from anyone who might overhear. Kev showed Eldet and Lyria the book.

"It's not exactly what we sent them in there for," Kev said. "But I think it's one of the books I was looking for in the Scholar's Tower library. So do we call that a success, or not?" Kev looked to Eldet, who was smiling.

He held up a hand, and in it were two bracelets, woven with colored twine and polished stone beads.

Lyria gasped and reached for the bracelets. "Those are mine! I made those!"

"The rats did get what I asked for," Eldet said. "*And* the book. I'd call that a huge success."

"Does that mean that my jewelry case is somewhere in the Flowermiller Cafe?" Lyria asked. Her face was lit with delight.

"Or somewhere in the boarding rooms above," Kev said. "Most likely that, since we heard the rats come down the stairs."

Lyria's delighted expression soon died down. "What do I do now? I still don't know how I would get my case back." Then her face lit with hope again. "Maybe Dinnan could help me with the other residents," she said. "Maybe that's why he showed up in your picture, Kev."

"Maybe he's the one who took it," Eldet said matter-of-factly. "It's not like he would have told you when you asked, if he were the thief after all."

"Oh, yes," said Lyria, looking to the ground. "I guess that's possible. Not Dinnan, though! He's always so nice. And I don't see why he would steal jewelry."

Eldet shrugged. "Just a thought."

A group of people arrived at the door of the eating house, holding cloaks and coats above their heads to block the rain, laughing and chatting as they passed by Kev and her friends in the doorway.

"I'll ask my ma if there's anything that can be done about your jewelry case now that we know it's somewhere in the Flowermiller Cafe," Eldet said. "She'll be able to help us."

"Are you going to tell her how we found this out?" Kev asked. "She might not be happy with the use you put your rat training to."

Eldet grimaced. "I'll think of something to tell her."

"Well, I'd like my rats back now, please," Kev said, holding out her hands. "I need to head home before it gets too late."

"Oh, yes," said Eldet, who'd had the rats riding in his pockets, happily munching on fish biscuits while they talked.

The three friends parted, and Kev walked home with a hand on her satchel, thinking about the book the rats had brought to her.

THE GLASSBLOWER'S
DRAWING

Saturday proved to be almost as rainy as Friday had been, but the rain was somewhat lighter and there were more dry spots between bouts of drizzle. After spending most of the previous day at home, Kev wanted a change of scenery. Ma felt the same way, and she loaded up the wagon with more of her wares, as well as Kev's younger siblings, to go to the Onami fair whether it was raining or not. Kev walked part of the way with them, but parted ways when they passed the square near Flowermiller Cafe. She had decided to finish her drawing in the warmth of the cafe, surrounded by the scent of fresh baked breads and cakes and with a warm mug of coffee.

Being so near the Scholar's Tower, the Flowermiller Cafe was fairly full with students bent over their books even on a weekend. Kev would have preferred to find a table that was tucked away in a corner or that melted away from notice in the surrounding tables, but unfortunately the best one she could snag was near a side wall and on the back aisle, near the serving counter and the back door. Though she knew people weren't really paying attention to her drawing as they walked past, she still felt self-conscious that people might look over her shoulder as she drew. She did her best to ignore that feeling and concentrate on her drawing.

She returned to the drawing of the glassblower's stall at the fair. When she'd stopped, she had only outlines of the people in the stall, and even though she'd mostly finished the focal point of the glassblower and her forge, she felt that this drawing wouldn't be done until the rest of the people in the scene were complete as well.

Kev started with the seller behind the stall table and filled in facial features, details of clothing, and the racks and shelves of glass items displayed behind her. One by one, she moved on to the other customers in the stall and the small group gathered around the glassblower's forge. With each person that she drew, she grew more confident, more sure of herself, as she sunk into the feeling of the pencil on paper and the curve of each line. Soon enough, it began to feel as if each feature, each ripple of fabric, were sprouting from her pencil of their own accord, as if Kev were just the doorway for their entrance to the world.

She kept drawing until her coffee grew cold next to her, and the last half of her pastry lay forgotten on her plate. She leaned down close to her page, and her shoulders began to ache from being hunched; her hand grew sore from gripping the pencil. When she finally came to the point where she would stop with her pencil sketch and move on to adding colors, she stopped and stretched, leaning back in her chair with her hands above her head. She looked out over the cafe as she stretched, letting her eyes focus on a different depth so they could rest too. She flinched as she saw an unwelcome familiar figure.

Yeran, Tanar's merchant friend, was standing at the serving counter waiting for his order from the cafe. The server set a plate on a small tray next to a cup of coffee, and Yeran took it and turned into the room. Kev hastily averted her eyes, not wanting to catch his notice.

She had assumed he would look for a table in the main room of the cafe, but when she looked back up, he had walked past her and to the swinging door leading to the stairs and the back landing where Kev and her friends had snuck in last night. He nudged the door open with his shoulder and disappeared up the stairs.

Kev's eyes widened. Yeran lodged here too?

She looked back down to her drawing of the glassblower's stall. Just before she'd seen Yeran in the cafe, she had finished drawing all the people in her scene. Now with rested eyes, she examined it. At the very edge of the picture, there was a group of three people, seen from the side. One was Mage Carrick Valaso, her teacher, which was easy to see. The other two were a bit harder to discern, but now that she had his face fresh in her mind, she could tell that the other two figures were Tanar and Yeran.

She hadn't thought much of it as she had finished her sketch. They were on the outside edge of the scene, and she knew she remembered seeing them at the glassblower's stall, so she thought they had probably just been in her mind from the other day.

Now, though, seeing Yeran go up the stairs to the lodging rooms above the Flowermiller Cafe, Kev wondered if it was more than a coincidence. She didn't recognize anybody else in the picture besides the glassblower herself and the seller at the booth. But Yeran lodged here, and he had been at the Onami fair on the day of the second thefts. Maybe she and Eldet were wrong, maybe Lyria's jewelry case being stolen was related to the thefts at the Onami fair after all, just not for the reasons they'd originally thought.

Looking at the picture, Kev wondered how many things they had gotten wrong. Seeing Yeran there next to Mage Valaso, with Tanar on their teacher's other side, Kev felt that she wouldn't be surprised if it were Tanar who was responsible for terrorizing the Onami craftspeople at the fair. And although Yeran had never seemed like more than an audience for Tanar's hate-filled words, it wouldn't surprise her either if he had willingly gone along with it. He certainly hadn't done anything to stop Tanar, first when her mother had had words with the mage driver's cart, and next at the fair when Tanar was trying to bully her away.

And then, what of Mage Valaso? What was his part in it? He

seemed like a good teacher when Kev set him apart from Tanar. But if he supported Tanar in his opinions and vitriolic words in secret, then he wasn't as good of a teacher as Kev thought. Why would they have been to the fair together? Maybe it was just a merchant thing that Kev didn't understand, to be friendly with mages. But Mage Valaso was a well-known mage, teaching non-magical students at the Scholar's Tower instead of teaching mages at the Mage Academy. Why was that? Did he have an interest in bound magic, or things like craftmagic found at the fair?

Now, with Kev's picture finished, it seemed that Mage Valaso, Tanar, and Yeran must be connected to it all somehow. And Kev wouldn't be surprised if Tanar were singling out Onami, or craft mages, or both, for bullying and intimidation. He would probably happy to be responsible for driving the entire Onami caravan out of Mirella early.

Kev found that she was gripping her pencil so tightly that her fingers were curled around it and her nails were digging into her palm. She loosened her grip and closed her sketchbook. She didn't know what to do now. Part of her was tempted to go up to the lodging rooms now, find Yeran, and demand Lyria's jewelry and tools back. But without all of the information, that would risk her coming across as a fool, and it could even be dangerous. At the very least, she might get herself kicked out of the Flowermiller Cafe if he denied it and she didn't have any proof. She didn't like the thought of losing a nice coffee and study spot for the rest of her years at the Scholar's Tower.

In a daze, Kev finished her pastry and cleared up her spot. Then, she wrote a note to Eldet, another one for Lyria, and left the cafe in search of the nearest messenger mage station.

The cool air was a relief after the warmth of the cafe, which had grown stifling after having been there awhile. Kev closed her jacket against the cool drizzle and wrapped her scarf an extra time around her neck. She donned her matching warm umber-colored wool hat and mittens, knitted for her by her ma, with a beautiful design of leaves and acorns curling around the hat and adorning the backs of the mittens. Thus prepared, she began the walk back home.

As she walked, she thought about her new suspicions about Yeran and Tanar. The book that the rats had brought her from the boarding rooms last night, was it Yeran's? Was he the one the rats had found Lyria's jewelry with? She hadn't had much time to look at the book the night before, but maybe there would be something inside that would help. She would look at it as soon as she got home.

Kev stopped at a small messenger mage shop on the next block down from the cafe and paid for her notes to be delivered. The notes did not contain details of what she had seen, but just a message that she wanted to talk to Eldet and Lyria as soon as possible about the cafe. The clerk at the mage's counter took Kev's notes and money and gave her a receipt and a promise that the mage would send her messages as soon as they came up in the queue. Depending on how busy it was and how many mages were on duty at any one time, the message might get delivered today or maybe tomorrow, but within two days was the usual guarantee. Kev hoped that Lyria would see it before school in two days.

Once home, Kev shed her damp clothes and hung them on hooks near the hearth before building up the fire and replacing the grate. The fire in the hearth had been left to burn down to coals. The house was quiet, so she assumed Da had headed to the docks sometime after Ma and Kev and the rest of the family had left for the Onami fair. That done, Kev bounded up the stairs to her room, grabbed the book, and checked the rat cage.

The rats did not appear to be in any of their beds, hidey holes, or pouches in their luxuriously appointed cage, so they must have stayed with Sayess on their way to the fair. Kev's little sister had taken a great liking to the rats, even more than their brothers had, which surprised Kev a little. She had been sure that Jaen or Kadan would have loved the rats as pets, and they did love them. But Sayess doted on them, cuddled them, and fed them all kinds of delicious kitchen scraps. Kev shook her head thinking of it. It was better that the rats had gone to the fair with Sayess; they would stay warmer in their carry pouch under the little girl's warm clothes than they would in the empty house.

Well-settled in a chair near the fire, Kev opened the book, "On the History of Free Magic and Bound Magic," and slowly leafed through its first pages. It appeared to be a typical volume of history, purporting to deal with the very beginnings of the topic and then progressing through developments through the years. She scanned the first pages with the table of contents and then flipped idly through the chapters. She looked more closely at the chapters that dealt strictly with bound magic, wondering if there might be something here that she could come back to for her own studies. But it didn't seem to tell her anything about Yeran and Tanar's possible motivations.

She wanted to ask the rats why they had brought her this book. Part of her wondered if it was only because they knew she had been looking for books on the topic. But if that were the case, why would the rats have risked dragging that book all the way down the hallway and stairs of a boarding house they'd broken into? Of course, the rats wouldn't be able to answer her, but she still thought that maybe their reaction to her questions would tell her what she needed to know. The main one being, did this book come from the same person who had taken Lyria's jewelry, and was that person Yeran?

The light drizzle outside suddenly opened up into a heavier downpour, and Kev pulled her shawl around her shoulders, feeling thankful to be inside. She hoped that her Ma and siblings had found some shelter at the fair with their cousins to keep them dry. Knowing Jaen and Kadan, though, they would be out in the middle aisles, enjoying the open space afforded by the lower atten-dance at the fair and frolicking in mud puddles. At least they had their rain jackets made of waxed linen fabric woven by her mother, and well-made boots.

Since the house was quiet, and with nothing else to be done at that moment, Kev flipped back to the front of the book and decided she would begin to read it. As she turned past the title page, something caught her eye. There, in the list of authors' names, was Mage Carrick Valaso! He was one of the authors of this work of history that had been singled out by the rats as something to do with Lyria's stolen jewelry case. Was it a coincidence? Or was there a reason that Yeran had a book written by their professor, and that the two had shown up in Kev's scrying drawing of the glassblower?

Kev took out her journal and began to make notes of everything from today that she would need to remember to tell her friends. Then she turned the page and began to read with excitement. Perhaps the book would have answers for her after all.

AN UNFAIR
ACCUSATION

Despite her notes sent to Eldet and Lyria, Kev didn't see either of them for the rest of the weekend. Runners from the messenger mage shop near her house delivered Eldet and Lyria's replies to Kev the morning after she sent them, both unable to meet with her that day. Eldet's note held an encouraging addition, mentioning that he was talking to his mother that day about their discoveries the other night. Kev was glad he seemed cheerful about it, because she worried that Eldet's ma would be upset with him for using the rats that way, and perhaps with Kev for letting him. She hoped he would think up some other explanation for how they discovered Lyria's thief.

Kev arrived warily to her History of Magic class on Monday. It would be the first time she would see Tanar, Yeran, or Mage Valaso since she'd seen them at the fair, except for Yeran's appearance at the cafe on Saturday. That morning, she had dutifully checked all the pockets, nooks, and crannies in all of her clothing to be sure the rats did not leave the house with her, and she gave them a lecture as they crunched their food happily in their cage. They just looked at her as if they didn't understand a word of what she was saying, as if they were normal rats simply interested in their mix of grains and seeds each morning.

"You'll be no help if Tanar sees you in the Scholar's Tower, do you understand?" she said. "I'll handle him on my own."

Still, she couldn't help laughing at the memory of him squirming and flailing at the fair as she walked into her classroom that morning. And the rats scrambling all over his legs had helped her get away when he'd been trying to pin her in place. So she couldn't completely blame them.

Kev had made sure to get to class early so she could choose a seat where she might escape Tanar's notice, and luckily only a few other students had arrived when she walked in. She sat one row back from a tall girl with blonde hair, hoping that others might take the places around them before Tanar could sit near her. What she really hoped was that he wouldn't want to sit near her at all.

Unfortunately, she didn't seem to have much luck, because as soon as Tanar arrived, his attention was focused on her. He saw her immediately and smirked before he took a seat. When Mage Valaso arrived and began to set up his notes at the podium at the front of class, Tanar left his seat and went to speak quietly to Mage Valaso. He spoke a few words, then pointed and stared right at Kev. Mage Valaso's gaze followed Tanar's gesture and he met Kev's eyes, then nodded. Tanar smirked at Kev again as he returned to his seat.

Kev sank in her seat. What had Tanar told him? And what would he do about it?

Right now, the answer appeared to be nothing, for Mage Valaso looked at the clock and then hurriedly prepared his notes and began his lecture.

She tried not to be distracted for the rest of the class hour, and she kept her gaze on her notes page, feeling too sheepish to look up at Mage Valaso. She didn't like to imagine what Tanar might have said about her.

At last, the moment she'd been dreading came. Just before the bells sounded, Mage Valaso finished his lecture and dismissed the class.

"Keveren Auberel?" he said uncertainly. When she met his eyes, he said, "May I speak with you briefly? It won't take long."

Kev nodded and gathered her things as the rest of the students filed out of the front and back doorways. She watched Tanar walk out with his head bent toward Yeran and imagined him congratulating himself for whatever his plan was. They both burst out into laughter as they left the room.

Kev approached Mage Valaso at the front of the room as it emptied. He nodded to her and cleared his throat. He fidgeted with the edges of his sleeves and his cheeks were slightly flushed. Kev thought he seemed nervous. Why?

"Good morning, Keveren. I've, uh, been asked to speak with you about some concerns with your behavior toward another student," he said.

"You mean Tanar?" Kev said glumly.

Mage Valaso flushed an even deeper red. "Yes, I suppose you saw him talking to me, although generally these matters are supposed to be kept confidential for the interests of all parties."

Kev wanted to roll her eyes, but she didn't think it would do her any favors in Mage Valaso's eyes. Instead she looked to the ground. She put a hand to her pack to reassure herself that the rats hadn't snuck into it at the last minute.

"Tanar reported that he has been experiencing some harassment from you and your friends," Mage Valaso said. "Now, that is a serious allegation, as I'm sure you're aware."

"Harassment?" Kev squeaked. She jerked her head up from the ground and looked at Mage Valaso in surprise. "How is he saying I've harassed him?" she asked.

Mage Valaso stared at Kev with his mouth half open, as if he didn't know what to think of her. That makes two of us, Kev thought. Did he really believe that she would harass someone?

He seemed to gather himself, and continued. "Well, he said that you have been following him unnecessarily throughout the city, and that you have targeted false reports against his family and their hired driver. And that you followed him at the Onami fair and made your pets attack him."

Kev glowered. "That's not fair, that's not how any of it happened," she said. "If anything, he's the one harassing me! At the fair— "

Mage Valaso cut her off by holding up his hand, palm out. "I'm not here to adjudicate the case today," he said. "And that's a good thing, because if it comes to it, it will require far more people and a proper hearing by the mage guard and before judges. But as the first witness to the complaint, it's my duty to counsel you on the consequences of any further actions in that vein. Now, I need to get to another class, as I'm sure you do. I hope to hear no more complaints of this kind, eh?" Mage Valaso glanced nervously out the door, where students had gathered waiting for them to leave the room.

"I'll make sure there are no more complaints," Kev said.

"Good. Well then," said Mage Valaso with a nod. He gathered his books and satchel and strode out of the room.

Kev followed after him, lost in thought. What in the world had just happened? How could Tanar say she had been harassing him when he had no proof? Yes, the thing with the rats had been unfortunate, but he had been blocking her from leaving in the first place, and she didn't tell the rats to do it.

She was still fuming when she found Lyria and Ferra at their usual spot in the art wing library.

"Woah, what's wrong?" Ferra said as soon as she saw Kev.

"Hello to you too," Kev said. "I haven't seen you for four days, and that's how you greet me?"

Ferra's eyes widened and she glanced at Lyria, who didn't seem to notice. She was packing away the tools at the work station.

"Sorry I asked," said Ferra. "But you really do look upset. Is there anything I can do to help?"

Kev sighed and slumped her shoulders. "I'm sorry to snap at

you. I just had the strangest thing happen. I'll tell you more outside."

"You know, I'm starting to like working at these stations," Lyria said, turning from the now tidied desk. "Even though it's not as portable, it's nice and quiet in here, and it's easy to pick up where I left off. Oh, what happened?" She had finally registered the dark expression on Kev's face.

"We'll talk about it outside," Ferra said in a dramatic whisper behind her hand, pretending that Kev couldn't hear her.

Kev laughed despite herself.

"Oh good," said Lyria, "I had something I wanted to talk about outside, too." She glanced meaningfully toward the checkout desk with her eyebrows raised. Kev looked and saw that Dinnan was working there again, as he usually seemed to be around this time of day.

"I have something to tell you about that too," Kev said.

"Oh, you mean what your note was about?" Lyria asked.

Kev nodded.

"Any news on your missing things?" Dinnan asked as Lyria turned in her keys and tools.

"Nothing," Lyria said, shaking her head woefully and looking down at the desk. Kev thought she noticed a little shake in her hands when she passed the keys over, and realized it was because Lyria still thought Dinnan was the most likely suspect for having taken them.

"Sorry to hear it," he said, turning away to hang up the keys. "Well, I hope they turn up."

Lyria thanked him and they left the library.

"I can't believe he would ask me that," Lyria said through gritted teeth when they'd gone down a floor. "Pretending to feel bad that I'm missing my things, when he's the one that took them!"

"You don't know it yet for sure," Ferra said.

"I'm pretty sure now," said Lyria. "That's what I wanted to tell both of you."

They finished their descent down the stairs to the courtyard and settled in their usual place under the tree. Kev was anxious to tell Lyria what she'd found out through her drawing and her sighting of Yeran at the cafe. It seemed that Lyria had latched on to Dinnan as the chief suspect, but Kev wasn't so sure. But first, she wanted to know what Lyria had found out that made her so certain that Dinnan was the one who had done it.

"What did you want to tell us about Dinnan?" Kev asked.

"Eldet was right," Lyria said, pulling a thin woven bag out of her pack. Inside the bag was a pile of fried dough balls, coated in sugar, from the fair. "Have some," she said, plucking one for herself. "When Eldet asked if Dinnan was a mage, and I said no, why would a mage work at a stupid job like the art library desk at the Scholar's Tower? Well, he is a mage. I checked the license directories yesterday."

"So you think he's the one Eldet sensed at the boarding house," Kev said.

Lyria shrugged. "Must be. And it explains why my bead was hot when I touched it, right before my things disappeared. He must be spying on us! Do you think he's trying to get us in trouble? I don't know why else he would be working here."

"He could just be a horrible mage," said Ferra. "Maybe he can't get work anywhere as a mage."

"He passed the license test," Lyria said with a shrug.

"I don't think it's him," Kev said.

Lyria's gaze snapped to Kev. "What? Why?"

"The mage thing must be a coincidence," she said. "Look at this." She withdrew her sketchbook from her pack and opened it to the page with her sketch of the glassblower's stall. She pointed to Tanar, Yeran, and Mage Valaso at the edge of the scene. "I saw Yeran at the Flowermiller Cafe two days ago. He was getting food and coffee, but when he got his tray, he went to the back, to the lodging rooms. He lives there too. And my sketch—well, if it worked right, anyway—my sketch is supposed to show me who stole from the glassblower's stall. I was holding this when I sketched it." She pulled on the cord around her neck to display the blown glass pendant she'd gotten there.

"May I see it?" Lyria asked, and took the sketchbook when Kev offered it to her. She traced her fingers across the page, examining the faces of each person in the picture. "They're right at the very edge," she murmured. "Are you sure it's meant to show them? Why not one of these other people?"

Kev pursed her lips. She didn't know if she could really be sure. But it all seemed to make too much sense.

"I don't know," she replied, truthfully. "I don't think I can truly know how my sketchmagic works until I study it more. But I do know that Tanar hates Onami people and the fair, and Yeran seems to agree."

"And they've got your mage teacher on their side?" Ferra asked, indicating Mage Valaso in the middle of the two boys.

Kev frowned at that. She didn't quite know what to think about Mage Valaso. Before she'd seen him talking to Tanar at the fair, she'd thought he was usually mildly annoyed by Tanar's interjections in class. "It seems so," she said, remembering this morning's conversation about harassment. She now told Ferra and Lyria what had happened that morning in class.

Lyria gasped, Ferra shook her head.

"Classic move," Ferra said. "He's accusing you before you can accuse him of anything. That way, nobody will believe you if you try to report him. It'll be your word against his."

Kev gaped at Ferra. She was right. Although the rats going after Tanar at the fair had been unfortunate, Kev didn't think that alone rose to the level of harassment. But if Tanar tried to take revenge on her for it, now Kev would have a hard time defending herself against him without seeming to prove herself a harasser. She glowered at the fried dough she'd just taken a bite of.

And now that Kev suspected that Tanar was the one behind all the thefts and harassment of the Onami sellers at the fair, she would look even worse if she tried to report him to anyone for it.

And she couldn't tell the Mage Guard that it was all based on a magic picture she'd drawn.

"So they are all connected, if it's them," Lyria said. "The thefts at the fair and the thefts at the cafe."

"But why is Mage Valaso involved?" Ferra said. "He wouldn't risk his mage license to support a couple of boys bullying the Onami."

"I thought about that," Kev said. She had been pondering the same question the last few days, as well as reading as much as she could of Mage Valaso's book on the history of magic. Although the book followed the conventional wisdom about the banning of bound magic, and the historical reasons for it, behind the words she could sense a sort of fascination with bound magic, subtle hints that the topic was of special interest to the author.

"I think Carrick Valaso is trying to study craftmagic," Kev said. "And that he might be trying to find out if craftmagic is really bound magic. The book that Yeran had in his lodging rooms, the one that the rats found, one of the authors is Mage Carrick Valaso. I wouldn't be surprised if Tanar had a copy of the book too. What if they're trying to steal craftmagic things so that they can get the makers in trouble for bound magic?"

Lyria looked at Kev with wide eyes, but Ferra was scowling. "I don't know. That's a lot to draw from just a few clues. I think we need more information. Why would any mage go to such lengths, when so many of them don't even think bound magic exists? Let alone craftmagic." She paused and pursed her lips thoughtfully. "But I do believe that Tanar would do it just to make Onami people feel uncomfortable. I only had to meet him once to see that he's a piece of work. Some merchants," she said, shaking her head.

"But you're a merchant," Lyria protested.

"My family are," said Ferra. "That's how I know how they can be. Besides, I did say *some* merchants, didn't I?"

"What do we do next then?" asked Lyria.

"Can you try to draw another picture, Kev?" Ferra asked.

"Maybe another of the Onami merchants this time. Or another one of the cafe, now that we know more?"

Kev bit her lip. She had struggled to get her mind in the right place for this picture, and started to feel a little nervous at the thought of having to produce another. "I can try," she said. "I'm still not exactly sure how to make it work."

Lyria smiled and put a hand on Kev's arm. "It's okay. Even if it doesn't work just right this time, the practice is the only way you figure out how it really works, in the end."

Kev smiled back at Lyria. Lyria's reassurance was strangely comforting. She was right about practice, Kev thought. She got good at drawing in the first place just by doing it all the time. Now that there was magic in it, that didn't change that she had to practice to get better.

"Thank you," she said to Lyria.

"And I've got some time this afternoon, so I'll see if I can track down Eldet and his ma," Ferra said. "I have some shopping to do at the fair anyway, so I can stop by the Outpost."

"If you don't find him, I'll see him tomorrow when he comes to my house to do more rat training," Kev said. She smiled wryly. "I'm sure he has plenty more ideas for them after last week."

Ferra rolled her eyes. "After last week, he should probably just take the rats to his apprenticeship master. It's one that deals with magical creatures, right? They're a lot more magical than he thought starting out."

"I suppose so," Kev said, but she didn't like the thought very much. What if the mage wanted to keep the rats to study them more? "Maybe I could go with him when he does," she said.

When their lunch hour was almost over, the three girls parted, all agreeing that they would meet again the next day with what news they could gather.

"Where was it that you checked to find out that Dinnan was a mage?" Kev asked, remembering Lyria's conversation from earlier.

"The mage license directories. They keep them at the Mage

Academy, in their archives. It's public, so anyone can ask to look at the records."

"How did you know that?" Ferra asked, giving Lyria a strange look.

Lyria blushed and looked down. "Oh, my family has had to make complaints against mages before. When I first moved into my room at the Landir Lodginghouses, there was one who thought he could drive me away. He said he shouldn't have to share a dining room with a filthy Onami vagrant."

"I never knew that!" Ferra said.

"It happened before I got to know you. Luckily, the Landir Lodginghouses handled it very well. And the mage guard handled the mage. He was disciplined for unbecoming behavior of a mage of his status."

"Serves him right," Kev said quietly.

And now she knew how she could find more information about Mage Carrick Valaso's career as a mage, she thought. She bid her friends goodbye and went on to her afternoon classes. She would have a lot to think about on her walk home today.

BULLIES

At the end of her second day of classes for the week, Kev left the Scholar's Tower feeling glum and slightly worried. Lyria and Ferra hadn't been in the art wing library when she'd gone to find them at the lunch hour, and they hadn't been in the courtyard either. She'd spent the whole evening in her room drawing the night before, and hadn't come away with much to show for it. Even so, she'd wanted to show the rough sketches to her friends to see what they thought. She'd tried to draw a scene from the cafe again, but this time she pictured Riskin's drawing case and pencils going missing. Instead of gaining any knowledge or insight into what happened with Riskin's art case, she ended up with another drawing of Dinnan passing through the cafe in the background, just like the first one she'd drawn for Lyria's jewelry. Perhaps she really did need one of Riskin's own pencils, or some other part of his art, to be able to focus her magic on the items that were stolen.

When she'd tried to draw another scene from the Onami fair, she'd barely been able to move past sketches. She used a little pouch of herbs given to her by Aunt Kalla and Uncle Vansal to focus her drawing. She had sketched their stall from her point of view when she'd stood there with them, behind the counter, and her ma ended up in the sketch too, to one side. The rest of it was looking out at the customers browsing the tables or walking by the stall out in the sunshine, but she was only able to get one customer fully filled out before her mind just simply seemed to stop working. Her ma had to remind her to go to sleep before it got too late, and Kev wanted to throw her pencils down to the floor in disgust.

So today she had been looking forward to seeing her friends even though she didn't have much news to tell them regarding her attempts at drawing new clues. She knew they would at least commiserate with her. Ferra was a painter, and had shared her own frustrations with difficult works before, and Lyria had already shown that she was understanding about such things too.

When Kev left the Scholar's Tower for the day by the front entrance, she felt wriggling in her satchel and sighed. The rats. Where had they come from? She stepped to the side onto the grass to be out of the way of the other foot traffic and lifted the top flap of her satchel to peek inside.

"What are you doing here?" she hissed.

Their whiskered noses wiggled at her. Turnip yawned.

"Fine. Just say in there so nobody sees you."

Green Bean stretched out fully so that her back feet grazed one side of the satchel, while her front feet pressed against the other, then curled back up around Turnip. Kev took that to mean they planned to continue napping.

As she closed the flap to the satchel again, she was shoved hard from the left, so that she went stumbling almost to the ground. She managed to stop herself with her hands before she fell on top of the satchel, which would have crushed the rats.

"Hey!" she said, and turned to find Tanar and Yeran sneering at her.

"I told you not to bring those things to the Tower," said Tanar, nodding toward her pack. He must have seen her talking to the rats.

"Oh, did you?" Kev said. "Then it's too bad for you that I

don't take your orders." She turned away from him and began to walk toward the street.

He grabbed her arm and dug his fingers in hard. On her other side, Yeran grabbed her other arm. He also took her pack off of her shoulder and gripped the top firmly, sealing it closed. Kev struggled, but their grips were tight, and Tanar was hissing in her ear now.

"You had better start taking my orders, witch," Tanar said. "Now stay quiet and listen, or Yeran will take care of the rats for good."

Kev tried to wrench her arm free again and twist toward Yeran, but Tanar's fingers dug even harder into her arm.

Tanar began to walk, pulling Kev along with him to toward the front gate of the school. None of the other students filing out of the buildings seemed to notice Kev's predicament. She bit her lip to keep from shouting, not sure if the rats had managed to escape her satchel or not. She knew they were some combination of magic and exceptionally sneaky, but she didn't know how much of each trait really contributed to their ability to show up anywhere. She couldn't take the risk that they were still in her satchel where Yeran could hurt them.

"I don't want to see your filthy Senemi hide in this school again, you hear that witch? After you go through that gate, don't come back." He and Yeran continued to propel her toward the gate as he spoke.

"You can't get away with this," Kev said.

Tanar snorted. "I don't need to get away with anything. I have connections who will make sure you do what I've told you."

Kev bit back a retort, knowing it would only anger Tanar more in this moment. She seethed inside, though. Twisting her head around, she scanned the crowd of students around her, wondering what would happen if she started to scream. But Yeran still clutched her satchel tightly, and she dared not do it.

They reached the gate, and Kev expected Tanar to release her at the threshold, but he kept going.

"What are you doing? Where are you taking me?"

"Shut up!" Tanar snapped. "I'm going to— "

But he never got to finish saying what he was going to do, because a shadow glided over them from above, and then a large, golden-scaled dragon circled around and landed before them in a rush of wind. It was Riki, Eldet's mother's dragon. Tanar and Yeran's grips loosened instantly, and Kev pulled herself free.

Riki rose on her hind legs before them, keeping her wings outstretched to look as large as she possibly could. She raised her nose in the air and let out a long call that echoed up and down the street. Then she lowered herself onto all fours to allow her rider to speak.

"Everything all right, Kev?" asked Dynet. Eldet was seated behind her and peering around her shoulder with a worried expression.

Kev opened her mouth, then shut it and scowled. She swung around to face Tanar and punched him in the mouth as hard as she could. With a wince, she pulled her hand back and shook it. That had hurt.

Tanar gasped and put a hand to his mouth and brought it away bleeding. While he was still reeling, Kev stepped forward and stomped on his foot, then pushed him backwards. He fell to the ground.

Kev turned to Yeran and held out her hand for her satchel. He gave it to her before rushing to help Tanar up.

She checked the satchel to be sure the rats were all right. They were cowering in the bottom, clearly braced to be swung about again. Their tense bodies relaxed when they saw Kev, and she gave them each a quick pet. "Stay there now, be good," she said, then turned to stand over Tanar.

"I have connections too," Kev said, looking down at him. "You'd better stop this nonsense, because I'm not going anywhere."

She turned and walked away, her legs threatening to wobble

right out from under her now that her rush of anger had subsided.

"Everything's all right now," Kev said, smiling at Eldet and his mother. But she could feel tears welling up behind her eyes. She needed to get home fast. "Mind if I get a ride with you?"

"We've got room for one more," Dynet said as Eldet extended a hand. They pulled Kev up onto Riki's back behind Eldet, and she held onto Eldet's waist.

"Kev, what happened?" Eldet asked in awe as the dragon's wings began to beat. "We were on our way to your house, but Riki said she saw you and that you needed help. Are you okay?"

"Mostly okay," Kev said. "I'll tell you when we get home."

Riki's wingbeats became too loud for them to talk, and Kev held tightly to Eldet as the dragon lifted first the front of its body, tilting them backwards, then the rest of it, into the air.

The dragon's back leveled out, and the wings locked into a smooth glide once they were up well above the streets of Mirella. Kev looked down at the tiny figures wandering the roads and wondered how Riki had even seen her. Dragons must have very good eyesight.

She didn't have long to wonder about much before Riki began circling for her landing in the square outside Kev's home. They tilted forward for a moment, then the powerful wings pumped as the dragon slowed herself to land gently on the cobblestones.

The dragon lowered her back and Kev slid to the ground as quickly as she could.

"Thank you," she managed and patted the dragon's side.

Eldet and Dynet followed, and after checking over the dragon's reins and saddle, Dynet turned to Kev, concerned.

"Are you truly all right, Keveren?" Dynet asked. "Riki said it looked like you were in trouble, and I have to say, it looked that way to me too."

Kev closed her eyes and tried to force the tears back in, but in the face of Dynet's kind concern, the emotions she'd been trying to hold back since the dragon picked her up came rushing out.

"I don't know what I ever did to him, but he won't leave me alone," Kev managed to get out between her tears.

"Was that Tanar again?" Eldet asked. "The one we saw at the fair?"

Kev nodded. "He said he was going to hurt the rats. I've never hit anyone before."

"Come here, sweetie," Dynet said, handing Kev a handkerchief and then enfolding her in her arms. "You did admirably. Sometimes a person earns the things that happen to them, even if you wished you hadn't had to hit him."

"Oh he definitely deserved it," Eldet said. "Did you see the way he was grabbing onto her arm?"

Dynet tsked. "We don't need to take such glee in it, Eldet."

From her vantage point over Dynet's shoulder, Kev giggled as Eldet nodded in an exaggerated way and mouthed, "Yes we do," in response.

"Let's go inside," said Dynet, turning toward Kev's home. "You'll want to tell your parents, and I don't want you to have to tell it more than once."

So they went into Kev's house and gathered with her parents around the table. Kev told about the incident in her class the day before with the supposed report to Mage Valaso, and then about today's bullying. Her mother gasped at the false report against Kev, and the story of Tanar's actions today brought her hands to her mouth. But when Kev was finished telling the story, her mother's face showed only fury.

"Why didn't you tell me about this before?" Kev's mother said.

Kev flinched and her mother's face softened.

"I'm not angry with you," said Ma, "I'm angry that it happened. You don't have to handle something like this on your own."

"It didn't seem like anything I couldn't handle at first," Kev said with a shrug. She hadn't mentioned her theories about Tanar's involvement with the fair thefts, just his claim to Mage Valaso that Kev was harassing him, and the incident at the fair with the rats. Throughout the conversation, the rats had sat calmly in her lap, letting her stroke them and bruxing their teeth in contentment. "I thought he was just being a jerk and if I ignored him, it would go away."

Ma pursed her lips and exchanged glances with Dynet. "I suppose that is advice I've given you often enough. But I'm proud of you for standing up to him today. I worry it won't be enough, though. Your father and I will go to the Scholar's Tower tomorrow and take it up with the administrators there."

Kev suddenly had a horrible thought. "Ma, I *punched* him. And I pushed him down! What if he reports me again for that?" She buried her face in her hands. She may as well have handed Tanar an excuse to blacken her name with the school even more.

Her mother put her arm around her. "We won't let that happen," she said. "But unfortunately, we can't let you go to class until this is sorted out."

Eyes wide, Kev opened her mouth to protest, but her mother put her hand up and shook her head.

Before Kev's mother could speak, Dynet chimed in. "Your mother's right dear," she said in her soothing voice. "Sometimes bullies give up when their victim stands up to them, but sometimes when they feel humiliated, they escalate. We need to keep you out of his path until we've determined which type of bully he'll be." Then she smiled, with an odd twinkle in her eye. "You said you've never punched anyone before?"

Kev shook her head.

"I'm impressed then. And the way you knocked him over before he got a chance to strike back was wonderful. If you'd ever like to refine your hand-to-hand combat skills, we'd welcome you in a class at the Outpost," Dynet said.

"Dynet," Kev's mother said in a scolding tone.

"It can be a good skill to have, even for non-riders," Dynet said. "We have lots of girls from all over the city come to take our classes. It can be useful in a pinch, and it's good exercise, too."

"I'll come to the class with you, if you like," Eldet said eagerly. "It's really fun. I'll teach you how to throw me!"

"You know how to fight?" Kev asked.

"Only a little bit," he said with a shrug. "It's never been one of my top priorities."

"Well," said Kev's ma, glancing back toward the hearth where Sayess, Jaen, and Kadan were all gathered, reading or working on knitting projects, and studiously pretending they weren't all listening to their conversation. "I suppose we need to get dinner started. Thank you Dynet, and thank Riki for me too."

Dynet rose and looked to Eldet. "I'll be back after dinnertime to pick you up, all right?"

Eldet nodded and waved goodbye to his ma before she left. Then he and Kev gathered up the rats and headed up to her room to begin on their original plans for the day—rat training.

"You know," said Eldet as they settled into their usual places, Kev on her bed, and him seated on the floor, "I think my ma's right, taking the fighting classes is a really good idea."

Kev stared at him. "Why?"

"Well, if we're going to be training the rats to track things and help solve mysteries, we'll probably end up in situations where knowing how to fight would be helpful." He said it in a very matter-of-fact tone, as if the conclusion that they would be solving more mysteries were foregone.

Kev continued to stare at Eldet, unsure what to say. Finally, she said, "I didn't think I was going to solve any more mysteries after I finished helping with Lyria's things."

"Oh, but I thought you liked it," Eldet said. He looked down at Green Bean, who had just clambered onto his lap and was sniffing at his pocket. As he spoke, Eldet pulled out his usual packet of fish biscuit treats for the rats and handed them out. "And you've got the perfect skills for it with your scrying drawings, and the rats are the perfect sidekicks. They'll be even better once they're fully trained."

"Fully trained?" Kev asked.

Eldet brightened. "Oh, yes. I forgot. Master Rithorn wants us to bring the rats to see him soon. Would you like to come? I could bring the rats myself too, if you're busy, as long as you're okay with it. But I thought you might like to come with me." His eyes widened and he gasped at a thought. "Oh, you could come with me tomorrow! Since you're staying home from your classes anyway."

At first, Kev scowled at the reminder of Tanar's assault on her, and that his actions were keeping her from going to school. But then she remembered that she had wanted to go to the Mage Academy soon and her mood cheered.

"That's right, I haven't got to tell you yet," Kev said, "about my drawing from this weekend. It has to do with Tanar too."

So she pulled out her sketchbook and laid the spread of the glassblower's stall before Eldet. Eldet listened as she explained that she had seen Yeran go up to the cafe lodging rooms, and her new theory about Tanar, Yeran, and Mage Valaso. He had heard the story of Mage Valaso talking to her about Tanar's false accusations of harassment downstairs. By the time she was finished, Eldet was staring at her, wide-eyed, looking like he was about to burst.

"Okay, what is it?" Kev asked. "I can tell you have something to say."

"Does Tanar know that you've found out about him?" The words seemed to come pouring from Eldet. "That could be why he's after you to leave the Scholar's Tower! And you said Mage Valaso was acting strange when he talked to you. Do you think Tanar told him that you suspect what they're doing? Yeran must have seen you."

Kev shook her head. "I really don't think he did," she said. "But I guess it's possible. I hadn't thought...I mean, I only did the drawing this weekend, and Tanar has been acting like this towards me for a while. But I think there's more. Remember the book the rats found?"

She showed Eldet the title page of the book, pointing to Mage Valaso's name as the main author.

"He studies bound magic," Kev said. "What if he's after craftmagic?"

"And he's using Tanar and Yeran's prejudice against Onami to get them to help him," Eldet whispered. He had taken the book and was flipping through it.

"I was thinking that I could look up Mage Valaso's license in the archives at the Mage Academy library," Kev said. "If I come with you tomorrow, will you help me?"

Eldet closed the book and grinned up at Kev. "Absolutely. Now, we'd better get to our rat training."

A Magical Creature
Workshop

aster Rithorn's workshop was located on the ground
floor at the back of the main building of the Mage
Academy. Kev had never imagined a place like this
would have existed in the Mage Academy, which she'd always
assumed would be full of arrogant, aloof mages bent over their
work in silence in austere but well-appointed rooms. But the
Mage Academy, now that she was here, reminded her a lot of the
Scholar's Tower. It was a school, after all, and there were students
Kev's age and even a bit younger, so it was loud and cheerful in
the common areas just like she was used to at her own school.

In Master Rithorn's workshop, the atmosphere was definitely
not calm and austere. Since Master Rithorn was a creature mage,
his workshop was full of all sorts of creatures. The spacious workshop room was full of enclosures of all kinds arranged in several
rows running up and down the room. Some of the enclosures
contained animals that Kev was familiar with, while others
seemed to be empty or housed creatures that she had never seen
before, even when she'd been kidnapped by Lady Orsta, a smug-
gler of magical creatures.

On one wall there was an aviary with an assortment of small
birds flitting about the cage and chirping. Near that aviary there

was a large wooden stand as big as a small tree with a very large parrot perched atop it. The parrot was bright red on its head and body, with green and blue feathers on its wings and a long red and blue tail. Its white and gray beak was large and curved downward in a hook shape. Kev stared at it as she passed at a safe distance, and the bird stared back. When it said, "Hello!" Kev jumped in surprise and looked to Eldet.

"It can talk?"

"She mostly mimics," Eldet answered. "That's Loret. It's short for Meriloret, but it's easier for her to say Loret. She's a green-winged macaw, from the tropical forests in the far south region across the seas. She was smuggled here by a sailor who befriended her, but he couldn't keep her. He changed ships to one that goes to cold places too often, and she isn't suited for that weather. So now she lives here. She's pretty friendly, but don't go close to her beak until you know her."

"Hi Loret, it's nice to meet you," Kev said with a nod in the parrot's direction.

"Do you have a treat?" Loret said in response. Kev laughed and looked to Eldet.

"I'd better give it to her, just in case," Eldet said. "Once you get to know her, she'll be good taking treats from you." He went to a cupboard near Loret's tree, and she clambered along the branches until she was perched on the one nearest Eldet. He emerged from the cupboard and handed a piece of dried fruit to the large bird, who took it astonishingly gently from his hand, then transferred it to one of her feet to hold it while she nibbled small pieces off with her beak.

"Thank you!" came the bird's cheerful voice as they walked away through the workshop toward the back wall.

At the back, there was a small, person-sized door next to a pair of larger storehouse-style doors that were bolted closed at the moment. Straw littered the floor before the large doors, and there was a spigot and a basin standing off to one side, with some dishes full of water arranged on the ground beneath it. Along the wall past the doors there lay a row of soft sleeping pads, and beyond that, a wall with many haphazardly placed shelves, all containing folded blankets or stuffed mats.

"Who sleeps there?" Kev asked.

"The cats and dogs and the like," Eldet answered. "They're probably all outside right now though, since it finally stopped raining."

"And the like?" Kev echoed.

"Oh, you know, like fairy lions and shadow foxes."

Kev didn't know. She'd heard of some magical creatures before, but not those two.

Eldet misinterpreted the reason for Kev's puzzled expression and added, "Since Master Rithorn's a creature mage, he makes sure they all get along."

Kev hoped that fairy lions and shadow foxes wouldn't be a problem for the rats.

Eldet led her through the smaller door to the yard outside. Immediately outside the doors there was a spacious flagstone patio, bordered on two sides by low stone walls. Past the patio was a grassy yard shaded by deciduous trees that had begun to drop their red and gold leaves to litter the ground below. In one corner, a small stand of pine trees stood above a carpet of brown needles.

Dogs and cats lounged in the sun or trotted around the yard, while several people who appeared to be students worked around the yard.

"Some of the other apprentices," Eldet supplied the information before Kev had a chance to ask. "I think Master Rithorn is around this way." He led her to the righthand side of the yard, through a gap in the stone wall and around a stand of bushes against the building.

A short, stocky man was bent down in the corner, dangling a feather on a string above a pile of squirming fur. As Kev got closer, she could see that it was a litter of kittens nestled behind a bed of flowers. One of the kittens erupted out of the pile of its siblings and grabbed onto the feather and the string, managing to suspend itself for several seconds before sliding off and falling back down to the pile.

At the sound of their footsteps, the man straightened and turned bearing a huge grin.

"Eldet! And you must be his friend Keveren," the man said, his grin somehow getting even wider. He held out his hand, and when Kev extended her own, he took it in both hands and gave it a vigorous shake. When he let go, he looked down with a grunt of surprise. One of the fuzzy kittens, light gray with darker gray stripes, had wobbled out of its nest and was still trying to catch the feather, which was still dangling from the stick that Master Rithorn had tucked under his arm. He scooped up the ball of fuzz and cupped it in his hands.

"This one's an adventurer, she is," he said, stroking the cat's head. "Nitha went to take a rest from her little ones for a bit, and this one wanted to go along. Didn't you?"

"It won't be long before they're running all over the place," Eldet said.

"Yes, but you'd better stay here for now," Master Rithorn said, addressing the kitten. He put her back in her garden nest with the others. "Ah, here's mama now."

A sleek gray cat slid along the wall and lay down alongside the pile of her kittens. The little things mewed and climbed over each other to reach their mama's belly to nurse. The mother cat, Nitha, gazed up at the humans with lidded eyes.

"Okay, Nitha, we'll give you some privacy," said Eldet's master. He turned to Kev and Eldet. "Let's go inside."

They followed him into the workshop and to a group of open tables surrounded by shelves. From across the room, Loret called "Hello!" in her gravelly bird voice.

"So you've brought your famous rats to meet me," said Master Rithorn. "I've heard a lot about them. Eldet says they're quite special."

"They're very smart," Kev said. "And sneaky," she couldn't help but add.

Rithorn chuckled. "As they should be. Rats survive on their sneakiness. So tell me about how you came to have them. Eldet mentioned Tara at the creature courts? May I see them?"

Kev opened her satchel and beckoned for the rats to come out. They allowed her to scoop them up and sat on her arm as she explained how she'd adopted them. Kev had happened to be at Tara's stall at the creature courts when a boy and his father had tried to surrender the rats to Tara, but Tara couldn't take them. The little boy hadn't wanted to give up the rats, but the father was making him do it. Although Tara sold pet rats through her stall at the courts, she had not had room for these two rats at the time, and when the father threatened to dump them, Kev had volunteered to take them. The boy and his father mentioned that the rats had been mage-raised, but it wasn't until later that Kev had come to understand what that truly meant, and she was still figuring out the extent of her rats' special talents and habits.

Master Rithorn pressed his lips together as he listened to Kev recount the day she got Green Bean and Turnip. He reached out a hand to stroke Green Bean, then held his hand palm up before the rat. Green Bean sniffed his hand, then crawled onto it. Rithorn cupped Green Bean in both hands and held her up so they were nose to nose.

"And Eldet says you two have been practicing some fetching and verbal commands," Master Rithorn commented. "May I see them work?"

Kev looked to Eldet, who was ready with supplies. He began taking out all kinds of things from the bag at his side and laying them on an open table nearby.

"It's mostly been Eldet working with them on that kind of stuff," Kev admitted. "I've had my hands full keeping them from following me to school!"

Rithorn chuckled. "They must like you very much."

Kev scratched the back of her head and smiled ruefully. "I guess they do," she said. "It's a lot of trouble though, making sure they don't get into any mischief while I'm just trying to take my classes."

"Ah, that it would be," Rithorn sympathized. He brought Green Bean around to the side of the table where Eldet had begun to organize his things and set her down. "Here, Green Bean," Master Rithorn addressed the rat, "Eldet has some activities for you. Would you care to demonstrate your considerable skill to an old man like me?" He put his hands on his hips and tilted his head to one side as he said it.

Eldet handed Kev a few rings of wooden beads, like bracelets, but smaller. They were each dyed a different color, a deep pink, blue, and yellow.

"Can you hide these around the workshop?" Eldet asked Kev. She nodded and took them.

The rats successfully retrieved the rings from their hiding places, each getting a turn with all three rings. Eldet put them through several similar trials involving different types of objects, with and without showing the rats the objects first, and with verbal and signed commands.

"Very nice," commented Master Rithorn after Eldet had run through his entire repertoire. "You've been spending a lot of time with them."

"Not at all," Eldet said, shaking his head. "When I tried to train them, they just teased me. So I stopped and just started telling them to do things. That worked a lot better."

Master Rithorn's eyebrows shot up. "So, their intelligence goes beyond that of even typical mage-raised creatures." He put a hand to his chin in thought. "Where *did* that child come across these as pets, I wonder? I don't know of any mages in Mirella doing this kind of work." He looked at Kev. "And you said Tara couldn't keep them? She must have recognized them for what they were."

"That's what she said," Kev responded.

Master Rithorn gazed at her thoughtfully. "She must have thought you'd be a good keeper for them."

"Oh, but she didn't know I was going to take them," Kev said, shaking her head. "I was there for other things." Tara had helped Kev learn enough about weyrdragons to find the one that had been kidnapped from the city of Areth.

"I can assure you, Tara would have taken them if absolutely needed. But since you took them, it clearly wasn't needed." He smiled at Turnip, who sat on the table before him eating one of Eldet's treats. "They are very well taken care of."

Kev blushed and waved a hand. "As if they would tolerate anything less," she said.

"You mentioned that it was a nuisance trying to keep them from following you to school."

"Yes," Kev said with a sigh. "I keep telling them they can't be seen there, that we'll get in trouble. But they don't seem to care."

"What if you stopped fighting it?" Master Rithorn said.

"What?"

"Yes. What if instead of trying to train them to stay home, you train them to be perfect traveling companions instead?"

"Just let them go everywhere with me?"

"With their intelligence and curious natures, I believe it will be the path of least resistance for you. They're clearly quite bonded to you as well, so it's likely they consider you part of their mischief."

"Mischief?"

"A fitting name for a group of rats, isn't it?"

Kev smiled at that. It was true. "I do already bring them with me most of the time anyway," she said. "Whether I choose it or not."

"The wonderful thing is, that once you start bringing them with you and training them to have manners, they will learn even more quickly and adapt to you as much as you will adapt to having them. I have something that may help, if you'll wait a moment."

He disappeared into a row of shelves and returned with a woven cloth rucksack.

"Now," he said, flopping the rucksack on the table. "This has special compartments, so it will allow you to carry your books and school things here." He lifted the rucksack and opened the top section, which was secured by a drawstring closure. "And then on the bottom here, and the sides, there are these other compartments. See how they're reinforced with sturdy wood? That's to keep the contents of the rest of the bag from squashing them."

The bottom of the bag was made up of more of the same fabric, but inside the lining on the bottom compartment there were panels of wood, so that when the pack was set down upright, the compartment didn't collapse. This compartment had side openings that were concealed by having one flap of fabric sewn over the other. The rats would be able to pry the two flaps apart and slide into the bottom compartment, but an observer looking at the bag would never think that there were openings there.

"They can also get into the side compartments from the bottom one," Master Rithorn added. "And there's a little pocket inside here for dry food, in case they're in there a long time. I never did come up with a solution for water, so you do have to let them come out for a drink from time to time."

"Wait, was this yours?" Eldet asked. He was holding Green Bean on one arm while he stroked the rat with his other hand. Green Bean lay stretched out to his full length on his belly, his arms dangling down the side of Eldet's arm.

"Well, it's my design," said Master Rithorn. "And yes, I have had pet rats many a time, though I haven't raised them using magic as some mages will. A shame their lives are so short, though." He tsked and shook his head. "But the rucksack works for, ahem, smuggling all kinds of animals of similar size, when one needs to transport a creature that they don't want being seen. So those of us who care for and rescue magical creatures have constructed quite a few versions of this rucksack. This one's brand new, and you may have it as a gift," he said. He fastened all the compartments and openings back up and presented the rucksack to Kev.

"Thank you, this is wonderful," she said. "Do you want to try it?" she asked the rats, and put the pack down on the table before Turnip. Eldet lowered Green Bean to the pack too. She perked up and sidled up to the pack, then nosed her way around the flaps of fabric and disappeared inside. Turnip did the same. Kev poked two more treats through the flaps and felt the rats' little hands grab them. Crunching ensued.

"As far as special training goes," Master Rithorn said, addressing Eldet. "Your time may be better spent just observing the rats and learning how they already communicate. I think you've suspected that for a while, no?"

Eldet nodded eagerly. "I thought so! They already showed us what they can do a little bit when— "he stopped before admitting that they'd broken into a cafe. "When they helped us find something that my friend lost," Eldet finished. "We just were never quite sure if they could really understand us."

"Well, if it were me, I would start from the assumption that they do, and work from there. Keveren, you will no doubt find them eager to cooperate the more you begin to communicate with them. And I mean real, two-way communication, so you must listen and attend to what they are trying to tell you, as well. If Tara has faith in you, then I do as well. The rats certainly trust you."

"Thank you," Kev said. She started transferring her books from her satchel to the new pack. When she was finished, she put the rucksack over her shoulders. She would be able to carry more in this compared to her satchel, which looped over only one shoulder.

"And Eldet," said Master Rithorn, "I have some book suggestions related to caring for mage-raised creatures. I'll make you a list."

Eldet nodded and began to pick up his training tools while Master Rithorn walked off to a desk in the corner of the room to write his list.

"Do you think you'll do it? Bring the rats with you everywhere?" Eldet asked, excitedly. He looked a bit wistful, Kev thought. He wished he could have the rats, Kev realized.

She smiled. "It seems I owe it to them," she said. "And I guess if he really thinks it'll make my life easier, it's worth a try."

Eldet grinned. "I thought so."

Kev squinted at him. "Did you know he was going to tell me all that? I thought you wanted to bring the rats here for your own studies."

Eldet blushed and stared at his feet. "I did talk about it with him a little bit before," he said. "He wanted to see if the rats were as mage-touched as it seemed from my stories of them before he said anything." He shrugged. "I guess now we know."

Kev shimmied her shoulders to feel the weight of the pack on her back while holding the fronts of the straps in each hand. It was still comfortable.

"I guess if they stay hidden when they absolutely must, it won't hurt for them to come with me. But won't they get bored hiding in my pack all the time?"

With a laugh, Eldet said, "I hardly think that's what they're going to be doing."

"I guess I'll have to trust them, like he said," Kev said hesitantly.

Master Rithorn returned with the list of books for Eldet, and the two thanked him again. Off across the room, Loret the green-winged macaw echoed their thanks with her own, "Thank you Master Rithorn."

They left his workshop as bells began to ring to mark the end of that hour's classes.

"I have to go to my class now," Eldet said, "but the library's on the way. Do you want to wait there until my class is over?"

Kev nodded eagerly and Eldet led the way to the Mage Academy library.

Mage Academy
Library

Eldet showed Kev to the library and left just as the last chime was ringing for the start of the next class hour. Unlike the Scholar's Tower, the Mage Academy building had been planned and built all at once on a single large plot of land that left them room to add wings and expand in a more orderly fashion than the haphazard jumble of buildings that made up the Scholar's Tower. Because of that, there was only one library at the Mage Academy. However, what the Mage Academy lacked in numbers of libraries, it made up for in the size of the library.

Kev stood on the ground floor of the library and tilted her head backwards to look up and up at the floors of shelves that seemed to stretch on forever. Grand curved staircases on either side of the sprawling main floor led the way up to the next floors, which boasted rows and rows of tall wooden shelves that looked down from the open balconies that ran around the perimeter of the room. Soft globes of mage light floated at intervals all throughout each floor, adding a warm glow to the beams of sunlight that reached in from the tall glass windows on the sides and ceiling of the grand space.

Luckily for Kev, a long desk stretched between the two staircases, and behind it several mages sat on stools waiting to help whoever may come to the desk in search of a book or document. Kev, though awed by the splendor of the library, no longer felt as intimidated by it as she would have before she'd started attending the Scholar's Tower. The libraries at the Scholar's Tower had intimidated her at first, until the librarians and her teachers had impressed upon her that the books were kept there for everybody to use, and that the librarians were there to help her find what she needed. So now she approached the front desk of the Mage Academy library eagerly and talked to the first librarian who caught her eye.

The librarian was a young woman dressed in deep blue mage's robes, as many academic mages liked to do. She smiled as Kev approached and set aside the pen and ink she had been using to write in a ledger.

"Good afternoon," the librarian greeted Kev.

"Hello," said Kev. "I'd like to look up a mage license. Can you tell me where to find those records?"

"Of course, they're right down that hallway, and you'll find the ledgers in the first room on the right."

Kev thanked her and set off in the direction the girl had pointed. Closer to the desk, she could now see that there were doors underneath the curved stairs that led on to other rooms of the library.

The room that Kev had been directed to was a more comfortable size than the yawning expanse of the main library floor. In the center of the room were several tables at standing height with thick, leather-bound books resting atop them. Lower, regular-sized tables with straight-backed wooden chairs populated the rest of the room that wasn't taken up by shelves. Around the perimeter of the room were shelves that contained books on the top half, and sets of sturdy wooden drawers on the bottom half. Each drawer was labeled with numbers and letters.

Kev approached one of the tall tables and opened the large book. She was happy to find that her suspicions were correct, and the book was a directory. Looking at the table of contents, she discovered that the books were organized first by year, and then by the last name of the mages who'd received their licenses that year. She sighed. She had no idea what year Mage Valaso would have gotten his license. But it made sense, the books must be added to each year as the licenses were awarded.

Well, she would just have to work backwards. She tried to guess how old Mage Valaso might be and at what age he might have gotten his license. There was no set age for mages to become licensed; it all depended on their level of education and when they started training under a master mage. In the end, she decided that she would be safe to skip the most recent five years, but didn't want to go too much farther than that without at least checking for his name in the book.

So, she drew a stray stool from one of the other tables and sat down to begin a careful look through the directories. She flipped to the V section of the directory under the corresponding year, and as she had suspected, did not find Mage Valaso's name listed. She flipped back several more pages until she came to the year previous to that. Still no Valaso. And on and on she went, checking the listings for his name.

Because the task was so monotonous, Kev's mind wandered to the issue of Tanar for almost the first time that day. She glowered when she imagined what his reaction might be to her absence from History of Magic class that morning. He would think he had won. She hoped that whatever her mother was doing, whoever she was talking to, would help the situation and not make it worse. Kev could only imagine how much more insufferable Tanar might get if he received anything like a slap on the hand and then continued to go about his business as normal. She just couldn't see how anything short of kicking him out of school would do her much good.

Well, if he turned out to be behind these Onami fair thefts, then Kev would have the last laugh when he was caught. And Mage Valaso too. It wasn't right for him to favor one student over another, even if they were helping him with some kind of project, and even if the project had been normal and didn't involve stealing things from others. If only Mage Valaso had given her a chance to speak when he'd warned her about Tanar's charges of harassment. She shook her head at herself. Who was she kidding? If Mage Valaso was working with Tanar and Yeran to steal craft-magic things from Onami, there was no way he would listen to Kev about Tanar's accusation being a lie.

With a deep breath, she attempted to banish the train of thought from her mind. She traced her finger down the page for another year's crop of mage licensees. No Valaso. She finally found his name in the entries for twenty-two years ago. Mage Valaso was older than she'd realized, she thought to herself, writing down the drawer number and letter combination.

When she found the drawer that contained the record of his license and related files, though, she discovered that not only was he about the age that she'd already thought him to be, but he'd received his mage license very early, at the age of fifteen. Only a couple years older than she was now. She brought the folder to one of the many low tables that ringed the room and spread out the file to study it.

There were several documents in the file, the first one being a list of all of the education that Mage Valaso had had leading up to his license. He'd been born in Mirella and attended a normal school until age nine, when he'd begun his training at the Mage Academy. The page listed all of the teachers he'd had and subjects he'd apprenticed in, and under which master mages. There were a lot of them, since he must have worked through the coursework very quickly to be licensed at the age of fifteen.

She flipped past that first page to look at what was behind it. The file included some work samples, letters from his master mages recommending his licensure, and then a copy of the license itself. Beyond that, Kev found another listing like the first page, which gave details of even more education that Valaso had taken part in after he'd been granted his license. Of course, she realized, he would have to submit records to keep his license current. And indeed, the page was incomplete, with room for more entries to be added as Mage Valaso submitted his information each year.

Kev ran her hand down the list. Mage Valaso had gone on to study for several years in the capital city of Areth, at the mage academy there. And then, the two most recent entries, accounting for the past four years besides this one, listed study at a college in Yennar Lei. Kev frowned when she saw the name. It was the name of a neighboring country to Arethia, but Kev couldn't quite remember which one it was from her geography lessons. Besides the seaports allowing trade on the coast to the far west, Arethia was a closed off country. The borders were very strictly controlled because of the ban on bound magic. That was one of the principal roles of the dragons and their riders, to patrol the borders. Only the Onami crossed them regularly, for it was normal and expected for them to travel.

Thinking of Arethia's ban on bound magic unlocked Kev's knowledge of Yennar Lei. Of course! It was the country to the south of Arethia, blocked by a natural border of tall mountains, that the rulers of Arethia had ceased all contact, negotiation, and trade with because of their heavy reliance on the use of bound magic.

Mage Valaso was studying bound magic, Kev thought. He had spent the last four years studying real bound magic in another country, one that Arethians supposedly couldn't travel to. Not over the southern border, at least.

After that entry on the list of his continuing education, there was one more sheet of paper. Kev turned to it and read.

It was a copy of a letter, received from the Arethian Board of Mages, scolding him for going against the approvals process to travel to Yennar Lei without permission. Despite the scolding, it granted him the right to return to Arethia provided he sign a contract promising that he would not practice magic of any kind for five years. In those five years, he would be required to teach classes to non-mage students at the Scholar's Tower in the basics of magic under the supervision of an appointed council of master mages in Mirella. During that time, his mage license would be suspended, and after fulfilling the terms of his punishment, he would be allowed to sit for specially designed exams to regain his license.

All for traveling to another country, Kev thought, bristling at the notion of being punished for what seemed like such a simple thing. It must be her Onami heritage, for they were free to cross borders without restrictions in all the countries where they roamed. In fact, the Onami caravan that was currently at the fair may well travel past the southern border. She couldn't remember if her parents had ever mentioned Yennar Lei when they talked about their past as Onami travelers, or when they talked about their family who still resided in the caravans. But since Onami couldn't be mages, the government of Arethia didn't bother them about the ban.

Kev leaned back in her chair. Craftmagic would change that, she thought. If it became known and studied, and found to be bound magic, the Onami might be put under more scrutiny, and allowed less freedom by Arethia.

So what was Mage Valaso doing? Or would his name only be Carrick Valaso, without his license? If he was supposed to stay away from all magic for the next five years, why was he meddling with craftmagic? And why would Tanar and Yeran help him? Did they know that his mage license was suspended?

Well, despite her inability to make sense of his reasons, Kev had found that Carrick Valaso had a connection to the subject of bound magic, and that fact in itself might help solidify the evidence of her sketch. She took out her notebook and made note of the file number for Valaso's license documents, and made notes of the dates of his education in Yennar Lei and his subsequent penalties. She would show Eldet's mother everything when she saw her today, and she would get the information where it needed to go so the dragon riders and the mage guard could solve the issue of the thefts at the Onami fair.

At a rustle and a squeak from Kev's pack, resting on the floor next to her chair, Kev remembered Master Rithorn's advice to make sure the rats had access to water often enough. This records room had been empty the entire time she'd been here, and it still was now, so she brought the pack up to the table and opened the small flap on the bottom back of the rucksack that allowed her to see the rats when they were in their hidden compartment.

"Are you two doing okay in there?" she whispered, looking around. The last thing she needed was for someone to come in at that moment and find her talking to herself. Then again, it wasn't like she knew anyone here, so maybe it wouldn't matter. And Master Rithorn clearly was okay with her having animals in the Mage Academy, so maybe it wouldn't matter if she got caught with them here.

The rats yawned, stretched, and sniffed the air in response to Kev's question. She wasn't sure what that meant, but she talked to them anyway. "I'll be done here soon, then we can take a break. Are you thirsty?"

Green Bean licked her lips and opened and closed her mouth. To Kev, that seemed like a yes.

"Okay, I'll find the nearest faucet. And Eldet's class is bound to be done soon," she said, looking up at the ceiling. Would she hear the bells chiming the hour here in the library?

As if in answer to her question, the distant sound of a bell beginning to chime floated to her ears.

"Well I guess that's that," she said. "Eldet will know the best place to get something to eat and drink around here. Can you stay put in there until we find a spot?"

The rats just stared at her.

"Or if you must run, or stretch, or whatever it is you do, just make sure you're not seen, all right? And return to the bag quietly."

The rats didn't move right away, but after Kev had gathered all the papers from the folder containing Valaso's license and returned it to the proper drawer, she came back to the desk to discover that the rats had vanished.

"When I said 'don't be seen,' I wasn't talking about me," she muttered under her breath.

Eldet was waiting for her near the main entrance of the library when she emerged from the records room. He was yawning when she approached.

"Fun class?" she asked.

Eldet sighed. "Magical Theory," he said. "I have to re-take it because my studies got interrupted when I took it at the academy in Areth," he said with a grimace. "It doesn't get better the second time around."

"Well here's something," Kev said, and told Eldet what she had found as they started walking.

After he'd heard everything Kev had found out about Carrick Valaso's mage license, he agreed that they should tell Eldet's mother, and the dragon riders, about Kev's drawing and her suspicions right away. She was planning to meet with Kev's mother at their house in the afternoon, when Eldet's classes were done, so they would tell her everything then.

Much to the rats' delight, Eldet brought them to an eating hall across the side street from the Mage Academy building. It was large enough to house scores of students, with long tables and benches filling most of the space, and a buffet at the front of the room. It had clearly been built to cater to the Mage Academy crowd, and since it was so big, nobody noticed when the rats reappeared to join Kev and sat in her lap, accepting crusts of bread and morsels of meat from her hearty beef stew.

After lunch, Eldet had two more classes for the day, so Kev spent the afternoon in a reading room in the great library, alternating between reading books for her classes and reading the two books she now had on bound magic. Mage Valaso's history of bound magic, she found to be measured and very informative. The first book she'd checked out from the Scholar's Tower library, "How to Avoid Bound Magic," devolved into paranoid ranting about the dangers of witches and "rejected mages," whatever that meant. It was clear the author held unfavorable views towards magic in general, and while Kev had hoped that there may be something useful hidden in the book, she quickly lost the patience to read it long enough to find any hidden gems.

Eldet found her there after his last class, her feet tucked up in the large leather chair and the rats curled in her lap, hidden from view by the large book she had propped up on her knees. Kev yawned when she saw him. The warmth of the library had made her drowsy.

"Ready?" Eldet asked. He reached out a hand to pet the rats, but instead they took it as an invitation to climb up his arms and perch on his shoulders. He laughed. "You can ride home that way if you want," Eldet said.

"Let's go," Kev said more cheerfully than she felt. She was worried to hear how her mother's complaint had gone at the Scholar's Tower, and she was worried to show her pictures to Dynet. She hadn't exactly told her parents that she'd been trying to find out who'd stolen Lyria's bag, and by extension, the other stolen things. But there was no avoiding it now.

As the two friends entered the cobblestone street under the rosy afternoon sun of autumn, Kev took a deep breath and held the straps of her rucksack. Whatever happened, she knew she could face it. Tanar wouldn't stop her from her studies at the Scholar's Tower, and she wouldn't let him stop the Onami from their fair, either.

Ferra's Quest

Kev and Eldet knew that his mother had arrived at Kev's house already by the dragon perched on its roof. Coming down the hill, they saw Riki's silhouette in the fading sunlight, which glowed orange over the bay and the waters of Lake Morna in the distance. By the time they reached Kev's house, there were only a few onlookers in the square peering up to see the dragon, who was studiously preening her wings and appeared not to notice. The rest of Kev's neighbors had either already gotten their fill of seeing the dragon, or were starting to get used to dragons visiting their neighborhood.

Inside, they found only Kev's mother and Dynet sitting by the hearth. Kev listened for the sounds of her brothers, sister, and father, but the house was quiet.

"Where is everybody?"

Kev's ma smiled. "Your father took your siblings out to get us some pasties and pies from the dock markets. They'll be back soon enough. I wanted to have some privacy while we talked about your school."

Kev grimaced even though she had known they would be having this talk upon her return.

"Well, Eldet and I will be going then," Dynet said, starting to rise from her chair.

"No!" said Eldet and Kev at the same time.

Dynet sat back down and gave her son a questioning look.

"We have something we need to show you," Eldet said. "It's about the market thieves. And about Tanar," he added.

His mother frowned and her brow wrinkled. She looked like she was about to say something, but then she nodded and beckoned to Eldet to sit in the chair next to her. The rats, who had still been perched on Eldet's shoulders after their walk home, slid down onto his lap, then to the floor, and scampered away, presumably to their cage.

"I guess it's been a long day for them," Kev said, taking a seat next to her mother, and next to the fire.

"Well," said her mother when everyone was seated. "I had a productive day at the Scholar's Tower," she said. Her expression was neutral.

"Is that...good?" Kev asked warily. She shuddered to imagine being one of the people who had to talk to her mother when she was angry, which she most definitely was in this case.

"It seems Tanar's father had already been in to make his own complaint before I arrived, so the school had a much different idea about what had happened." Her eyes narrowed at this comment and she smoothed the fabric of her skirt on her lap. "I was able to talk them into seeing sense about acting on the Polorelm family's information without conducting a proper investigation first. They are quite interested to hear more about your side, Kev."

Kev shivered. "You mean they still don't believe me?" she asked. "How long does an investigation take?" The idea of attending classes with Tanar while an investigation was still ongoing made Kev's stomach drop. "Maybe I should just take this class next semester."

"That's a possibility," her mother said with a nod, her voice softer now. "I can't imagine that your learning will be able to continue uninterrupted under the circumstances."

"Don't worry," said Dynet. "It's not unusual to take a class again. And the Scholar's Tower administration won't be able to ignore my and Riki's testimony as witness to Tanar's behavior."

"So I just have to drop out of class, and he gets to keep taking it just like he wanted? Then he's won!" Kev threw her hands up and flopped back in her chair.

"But Kev, what about your pictures?" Eldet said. "If he gets in trouble for that, he won't be able to keep taking classes. Not to mention Mr. Valaso...you might not have a class to come back to!"

Kev stared at Eldet open-mouthed. She hadn't thought that far through the implications of what she'd found, if it were all true.

Both mothers turned and looked at Kev, questions playing in their eyes.

"What pictures?" her ma said, raising an eyebrow. She knew of Kev's skill with drawing—her craftmagic skill—but Kev hadn't told her about her recent attempts at using it for finding things.

"There's, um, kind of a lot to explain," Kev said. "I was helping Ferra's friend, Lyria, find her jewelry-making case that was stolen. I did a drawing for her, but it didn't help. And then we thought it was connected to all of the things getting stolen at the fair."

She showed her drawing of the glassblower's stall to her ma and Dynet, and explained how she'd seen Tanar, Yeran, and Mage Valaso at the stall on the same night that things had been stolen from it. She mentioned seeing Yeran at the Flowermiller Cafe without mentioning that she, Eldet, and Lyria had broken into it, or that they'd sent the rats in looking for things.

As she began to talk about Mage Valaso and her suspicions of him working with Tanar and Yeran, Eldet's mother put a hand up to stop her.

"May I see the drawing a bit more closely?" she asked.

Kev handed her the sketchbook, open to that page.

She examined the drawing and smiled. "You did well in capturing the thieves in this scene," she said. "But they're not who you think they are." Looking up, she continued "I can definitely see why you came to the conclusions you did, but I can say with certainty that Tanar and your professor are not involved. The mage guard and the dragon riders just today caught the group of thieves who had been targeting the fair. See here?"

She lay the book on the low table in the center of all the chairs and indicated a group of two young men and one young woman standing near the glassblowing forge. At first glance, they appeared to be watching the demonstration, just like the rest of the people in Kev's scene. But upon closer inspection, Kev could now see that the woman and one of the men were looking past the glassblower, and the other young man was gripping a large empty sack at his side. Dynet tapped on the group.

"These are three of them, but not all by any means. There was a fairly large thieves' ring who were stealing items from the fair and selling them at the dock markets or loading them into a ship at the harbor. We've confirmed they were the thieves for sure, because the mage guard seized the ship and has recovered a large number of the missing items."

Kev felt a warm glow and at the same time, a sense of dismay. Her drawing had worked! Yet, she had gotten it all wrong about Tanar.

"So that explains why Tanar and Yeran were at the very edge of the scene," Kev said quietly to herself, tracing her gaze around her own drawing as if it were new. "And that explains why my other drawings didn't have them in them!"

She flipped to two other drawings she'd started of the fair and immediately saw that at least one of the three thieves from her first picture were included in the subsequent sketches. Dynet looked them over and pointed out two more of the known thieves' group.

Then she scowled. "So Mage Valaso is just friends with Tanar and Yeran? Ugh. Is he the only one who teaches that class?"

Dynet and her mother laughed. "I wouldn't worry too much about that," Dynet said. "When we spoke to him today, he had nothing kind to say about Tanar, and he apologized for making you think that he was meaning to discipline you. He was attempting to follow the protocols at the Scholar's Tower regarding reports like Tanar's, but since he is rather new to teaching there, he delivered the message a little awkwardly. He meant to warn you of Tanar's report so you could guard against it happening again."

"So then why were they together at the fair?" Kev asked, still feeling sour.

"Perhaps they simply ran into each other there," Ma said with a laugh.

"So, does this mean the whole thing is solved?" Eldet said, sounding somewhat disappointed. "We didn't help at all?" His shoulders slumped.

"Eldet," his mother said in a scolding tone, "the best way for you to help, with anything, is to focus on finishing your education. And you did help plenty, the dragons highly appreciate your grooming and bathing skills."

Eldet scowled at his mom and sighed.

"Can we check the things that the thieves stole to see if Lyria's jewelry case is with them?" Kev said, suddenly brightening. Lyria might be able to get her things back in time to sell more of them at the fair!

Dynet nodded. "Yes, I'll give you the details to pass along to her so she can come look at what was recovered."

Kev took her sketchbook back and paged through it as her mother and Dynet chatted quietly about the Onami Fair thefts. Her mother was relieved to hear that Aunt Kalla and Uncle Vansal had been among the makers who got their things back. Kev flipped backwards through her sketchbook, stopping at one of the pictures she'd drawn of the Flowermiller Cafe. She'd been wrong about what she'd seen in the pictures she'd drawn of the Onami Fair. What if she'd been wrong about the pictures at the cafe, too? But she didn't see any of the thieves' faces in these pictures.

A loud, frantic pounding on the front door interrupted their quiet chatting. Kev jumped up to answer it, ready to scold her brothers when they came in the door. They always liked to play games with the door, like pretending they were a delivery person and then surprising whoever answered it by jumping out of hiding. She was not impressed.

But when the door opened, it wasn't Kev's brothers as she'd expected. It was Ferra. She rushed into the house, looking around everywhere as if she expected to find someone else there.

"Is Lyria here?" she asked, panting.

Kev stared at Ferra for a moment, her mouth half open, then finally shook her head. "No, I haven't seen her since we met for lunch two days ago."

Ferra threw her head back and groaned. "That's the last time I saw her, too! Her parents came to me at the lodging house to see if she'd been staying in her room there. She hasn't been home to their wagon in three days!" She was still panting heavily, and she put a hand to her forehead and shook herself.

Eldet's mother strode across the room and took hold of Ferra's hands. "Don't worry, child. We can help," she said. "Where are her parents now? I'll go with Riki and talk to them. The riders can start a search."

"I don't know, they must have gone back to the fair, to their wagon."

With a nod, Dynet gestured to Eldet. "Come on, I'll drop you at the Outpost when I go to inform the other riders."

"Can I—can I stay here?" Eldet asked. "I just, me and Kev had some more rat training ideas after meeting with Master Rithorn today."

"I may not be able to return later," Dynet said. "You'll have to walk home."

"It's okay!" Eldet said. "Kev will walk me part of the way."

"If it gets too late, he can stay here," Kev's ma said warmly. "You too, Ferra. Let's get you some tea. And I know Mister

Auberel is bringing enough food home from the markets to feed an army, so two guests for dinner will be just fine."

Ferra took another shuddering breath and nodded at Kev's mother's words.

"Let's go upstairs," Kev said and looked to her ma.

Her mother nodded. "I'll bring the tea up to your room."

The three youths clattered up the stairs and filed into Kev's bedroom. Kev let Ferra sit at the head of the bed, while she took the foot of the bed and Eldet sat cross-legged on the floor.

The rats crept out of their cage curiously, and seemed to sense that Ferra could use some comforting. They both nudged at her hands until she scooped them up and settled them in her lap.

"What could have happened?" Ferra said. "Something must have happened to her. She wouldn't have run away, no matter what the dumb old biddies at the lodginghouse were saying. Just because she's Onami they think she'd just disappear." Ferra scowled into her lap.

"You truly didn't see her anymore the other day, after we talked in the courtyard?" Kev asked.

"Just in our next class," Ferra said. "But after that, we have different classes in the afternoon. I thought we were going to meet in the library again the next day, but she never came, so I just thought she must have been sick or something."

Kev thought back to the last time she'd seen Lyria and Ferra. They had been talking about Kev's drawings of Tanar. What if Lyria had confronted him about her jewelry case? But no, Lyria wouldn't do something like that. Would she? And she hadn't heard about Kev's ordeal with him yet, so she wouldn't know how truly hateful and vindictive he could be. What if he had hurt her? Especially now, knowing that Kev's suspicions about Tanar and Yeran had been wrong, a knot formed in her stomach. What if something had happened to Lyria because of her?

"The last time I was with you and her," Kev said to Ferra, "I was showing you my drawings of Tanar and Yeran and Mage

Valaso at the fair. Would she have tried to confront Tanar about her jewelry case?"

"She's way too shy for that," Ferra said, shaking her head. Her gasping breaths had calmed now and her expression grew thoughtful. "She did seem preoccupied after that, though. At least, I think so. She was pretty quiet in class, but it was a lecture, so we didn't talk much anyway."

As they spoke, Eldet was busy rummaging around in his school pack. Now, he emerged from his digging holding up a cloth pouch.

"I know what we're going to do," he said.

Kev and Ferra's heads swung to face him.

"What is that?" Ferra asked.

Kev sighed. "Fish biscuits."

Ferra jumped as the rats suddenly came awake and scrambled out of her lap at the sight of the pouch in Eldet's hand.

"That's right, who's a good rat?" Eldet said with a huge grin. He opened the pouch and distributed a rat-sized biscuit to each rat.

"Eldet, we can't," Kev said.

"Can't what?" Ferra asked, looking back and forth between Kev and Eldet. "What can't we do?"

"We're going to have the rats track Lyria's scent!" Eldet said. "They'll bring us straight to her. Won't you?"

"Shhh," Kev said, glancing towards the door. Her mother hadn't arrived with the tea she'd promised to Ferra yet. "Don't let my ma hear you. She'd never let us go off for that."

As if her words had summoned her, Kev heard her mother's footsteps on the stairs, along with the clinking of tea mugs on a tray. She appeared in the doorway and rested the tray carefully on the bed between Ferra and Kev.

"Your da and the others will be back with our dinner pretty soon, I would think. I'll call you down when it's time," she said, smiling warmly at Kev and her friends.

After she had left, Eldet continued on his track. "Kev, do you still have the bracelet that Lyria gave you to do your drawings?"

"Yes, but my ma's never going to let me leave tonight," Kev said. "Not after the thing with Tanar. And I'm not breaking into anywhere else," she hissed. "Your ma and the other riders will find her. It will be fine."

"But we have to help if we can," Eldet said.

"Well then why don't you go run it by your mother?" Kev said.

Eldet laughed. "Oh my ma would never let me do it," he said. "Besides, it's going to take ages for the riders to organize a search. They'll want to wait for the commander to assign the right riders, then they'll go talk to Lyria's parents, then they'll interview anyone else who saw her, probably check all the places her parents and Ferra have already checked, just for good measure. It'll be much faster if we find her first and then tell them where to look."

Kev gaped at him. "Is that really how it is?" She knew the mage guard could be tied up in bureaucracy sometimes, but she'd always pictured the dragon riders being a step above that.

He shrugged. "Sometimes. I mean it makes sense to do it all that way for most things. But I think the rats will be faster for this."

Downstairs, Kev heard the front door rattle open and the sound of four pairs of clomping feet enter the house. Her da and siblings had returned.

"There's no way I'm leaving the house tonight," Kev said again. "My ma is too worried about Tanar. Plus, it's dinner time. She's not going to let either of you miss dinner either."

Eldet looked like he was about to burst. "Can I just borrow the rats tonight?" he asked.

Kev opened her mouth, about to say that it wouldn't be safe for them, but she changed her mind. The rats could probably handle themselves better than she could. "It's up to the rats," she said. "But you have to explain it to them fully."

"I'll go too," Ferra said. "After dinner, though. I don't want your ma to worry. Besides, that smells amazing."

Kev didn't blame her; the smell of meat pies and cheese biscuits had just wafted up the stairs and reached her nose as well.

"Okay, ratties," Eldet said, leaning down to the rats, who were now in his lap, eagerly sniffing the pouch for more treats, "have you been listening? Here's what we're going to do."

Kev shook her head and headed down to dinner. Of course the rats would do it. She tried to ignore the pit in her stomach telling her that maybe she should go too. Lyria was missing, and she wasn't doing anything. But she knew that what she'd said about her mother was true; she wouldn't let Kev out of her sight tonight. The dragon riders were searching for Lyria, and soon Eldet and Ferra would be too, with the help of Kev's rats. She had to accept that it would be enough.

Rat Trackers

To Kev's great surprise, Eldet and Ferra managed to make it through dinner without acting as if anything were out of the ordinary. The intensity and eagerness that Kev had seen upstairs, when Eldet was explaining his plans to the rats, had disappeared, and he looked relaxed as he ate and joked with Kev's brothers. Ferra, too, hid her anticipation well, but she remained quiet throughout most of the meal. Of course, knowing that her friend was missing, nobody questioned her reticence this evening.

Kev, on the other hand, felt on edge and could not sit still. Her knee bounced under the table, and she kept playing with her fingers in her lap. Perhaps Eldet was able to keep his calm because he knew he had a plan, while Kev knew she had to remain home, doing nothing.

When dinner was finally over, Eldet and Ferra excused themselves to walk to the Outpost despite Kev's parents' offers to let them stay the night. Kev waved them off, sending a silent goodbye to Green Bean and Turnip, who were hidden in her new rucksack that Ferra now wore on her back.

Though Kev's mother seemed to want to talk to her more about her plans for school the next day and her meetings regarding Tanar, Kev couldn't bear the thought of more conversation. She pled exhaustion and climbed the stairs to her room.

It felt empty without the rats. Even though they had been gone on their own adventures with her ma or siblings on plenty of occasions, they had always been back home in their cage by bedtime. Knowing that they were off on a possibly dangerous search made Kev feel lonelier without them here.

What had happened to Lyria? She had no reason to run away from her family, or her school, or anything like that, so something must have happened. Was it related to her missing jewelry case, or Tanar, or had she just had completely unrelated bad luck?

Kev flopped back on her bed and pounded on her mattress with her feet and clenched fists. She bit her lip to resist the urge to roar in frustration. She lay there a moment, breathing hard, tears welling at the corners of her eyes. She wanted to *do* something. Then she let out a small, "oh." She knew what she could do.

When she sat up, she got out her sketchbook and pencils and flipped to an open page. She began to draw.

She didn't stop to think about what she would draw, she simply let her pencil flow across the page and let herself feel the full weight of her frustration, fear, and anger at her friend's disappearance. She let her mind wander over every detail of the last several days, every word spoken by Lyria, her friends, all the people they'd talked to.

On the page, a form began to take shape. It was a girl lying sprawled across a sofa or a chair, her arms and legs askew, her head flopped to one side. Kev's stomach swirled with worry. This didn't look good.

The face formed under Kev's pencil strokes. The girl's eyes were closed, her mouth open slightly. Her hair was fanned out beneath her, bedraggled. Kev kept drawing, filling in the eyebrows, the nose, the ears. There was no question of it, the girl pictured was Lyria, and she was unconscious.

Kev bent further over her page and continued drawing, trying to fill in the details around Lyria's fallen form. She was on a sofa, but where? Bunched up blankets, flattened pillows, a fallen pitcher on a table nearby all emerged to fill up the room, but there was nothing that would tell Kev where the room was or who had done this.

"Come on, is there someone there with you?" Kev whispered, but she couldn't get her hands to sketch another person. The room was empty.

Kev slapped her pencil down on the page and threw her head back with a groan. What use was having sketchmagic if she couldn't get it to work? More and more, it seemed like her past successful attempts at using her sketchmagic to find the weyr-dragon had simply been a fluke. She had been lucky—simple beginner's luck.

But no, her drawing of the glassblower's stall, and her other drawings of the Onami fair, had been right. She had just inter-preted them wrong. She sat back up and looked at the picture in her lap. Poor Lyria.

Kev turned her sketchbook back a page, partly to get the picture of Lyria, unconscious and hurt, out of her view, and partly to look at her pictures from the fair. She touched a hand to the people Dynet had identified as the thieves. The sketches had been right, Kev just hadn't seen it because she'd focused on Tanar. Focused.

She flipped farther back to the sketch of the glassblower's stall.

There was Tanar, Yeran, Mage Valaso. Though they were at the edge of the page, Kev had drawn them in great detail. Their features were clear and sharp. She'd been focused on them. She looked at the other people in the sketch. The glassblower was just as clear, but others in the stall, whether shopping or watching the glassblowing demonstration, weren't drawn in such detail. As if Kev's sketchmagic knew they were unimportant. The three thieves, though, the ones Dynet had pointed out, were detailed and clear too, just like Tanar was.

Kev *had* gotten it right. She was more sure of it now, seeing that even then, before Dynet had pointed them out, she'd given more attention to the sketches of the real thieves. It had just been muddied up because she'd seen Tanar at the fair that day, at the glassblower's stall itself, and so she'd given him more detail too.

Suddenly, a thought hit her, and she froze. If the Onami fair sketches had been right all along, what about the ones she'd done of the Flowermiller Cafe?

With a trembling hand, she flipped farther back in her sketchbook.

Dinnan. Every sketch she'd made of the cafe included Dinnan. From the very first one, they had him. Even though the sketches depicted many people in the cafe, like the bakers, the servers, and the other customers, Dinnan was the most detailed figure in every image.

They'd thought it was just because he lived in the lodging rooms above the cafe, that he happened to be in the pictures. They'd believed him when he said he didn't know anything about the jewelry case being stolen, when he said he'd talked to the cafe owner, and when he'd said to let him know if he could provide any more help.

At that thought, Kev sat up straight. What if Lyria had gone to talk to Dinnan again? The last time Kev had seen her, she'd told Lyria that she thought Tanar and Yeran were responsible for the Onami fair thefts, and that Yeran lived above the cafe too. Could Lyria have tried to go to Dinnan for help with Yeran?

Whatever had happened, Kev now knew she had to tell the dragon riders. They had to check the Flowermiller Cafe, they had to know to talk to Dinnan.

She shook her ma and da awake, keeping as quiet as she could. She didn't want to wake her siblings. She explained her idea to her parents as briefly as she could.

"We need to get a message to the dragon riders, and I need to go to the Flowermiller Cafe," she said when she had finished.

Her mother and father looked at each other as Kev held her breath. Then, her mother threw the blankets off of her and stepped into her slippers.

"You stay here with the kids," Ma said to her father, "I'll go with Kev to the messenger's and the cafe."

Da nodded and gave Kev a smile.

"Good work, Kev," he said, and lay back down.

Ma went to her wardrobe and then glanced back at Kev. "I'll meet you downstairs," she said and made a shooing motion with her hand. Kev backed out of the room and closed the door.

"Now," said Kev's mother as she came down the stairs, dressed in her knit leggings, a long tunic dress, and her coat, "We need to get the message to the dragon riders as quickly as possible. Then we'll see if there's anything we can do at the cafe."

Kev nodded and trotted with her mother out the front door.

"And what about Eldet and Ferra," her mother asked once they were out on the quiet street. "Where did they go? We need to get a message to them as well."

"I, um..." Kev trailed off. She'd left that part out of it, not wanting her mother to know about Eldet's plan with the rats.

Her mother put her hands on her hips. "They were up to something, I know it. I can't see why Eldet would have seemed so happy at dinner, otherwise."

Kev couldn't help but chuckle. Eldet *had* been a little bit too excited to use the rats as trackers. She sighed and with a rueful grin, told her mother about Eldet's idea.

"But I'm not sure where they started," Kev said. "Maybe the Scholar's Tower? That's the last place Ferra or I saw her."

Her mother looked thoughtful. "Well, we'll have to settle for sending a message to Dynet. I hope Eldet has some sense and goes to his mother if they find anything of use."

They were walking briskly now, and when they reached the closest messenger mage station, Kev's mother went in and hastily dictated a message to the unfortunate young mage who had the night shift.

They didn't have to worry about Eldet and Ferra for long, because they found them at the Flowermiller Cafe. Despite the late hour, the whole cafe was alight with mage lights and full of people. Dragons filled the square outside the cafe and perched on the roofs of shops nearby. Kev broke into a run when she saw the scene, stumbling to a stop in front of two dragon riders who moved to block her path when they saw her coming towards the cafe. They stood next to their dragons, who effectively blocked off this entire side of the square.

"Is Lyria in there?" she asked.

The two riders exchanged glances before one spoke.

"I'm sorry, but we can't let anyone through right now," said the dragon rider. She shot a worried glance at Kev, then at her mother, who was just catching up.

"I need to get a message to Dynet," Kev said, hoping that mentioning another rider would help.

The two dragon riders were saved from having to decide what to do when Eldet and Ferra ran over from the front door of the cafe.

"I need to talk to your ma," Kev said.

"I'll get her," Eldet said with a nod, and ran off.

"Can they come through?" Ferra asked the riders who blocked the way. "We need their help. Dynet will confirm it, I swear."

The first rider pursed her lips and shot a sidelong glance at her partner. She looked like she was about to refuse, but then her dragon lifted his head and nuzzled her arm. She turned her head toward the dragon, as if she were listening to something, then nodded.

"Dynet says you can pass," she said, and she and her dragon moved aside.

Kev and her mother followed Ferra to the cafe, and when they arrived inside, Eldet was there with his mother at one of the cafe tables. The room was scattered with other people, many of whom Kev assumed to be the other tenants of the upstairs rooms. Behind the front counter, a pair of mage guards talked in low voices with Mrs. Flowermiller.

"I think it's Dinnan," Kev said as soon as she was seated at the table with Dynet, Eldet, Ferra, and her mother. She spread open her sketchbook, which she had been clutching under her arm the whole way here. She showed them the previous drawings and explained how they'd thought Dinnan was only in the background of the drawings by coincidence.

"But then I realized that I made the same mistake with these pictures as I did with the ones from the fair," Kev said. "I didn't focus on the right things."

"Well, we think you're right," Dynet said, looking somber. "Unfortunately, Dinnan is nowhere to be found, and neither is Lyria."

"Can I see his room?" Kev said, hoping that it would tell her something. She flipped to her most recent drawing, the one she'd made that night. She touched her hand to the picture where Lyria's arm draped over the side of the sofa. "I thought she'd be here."

Dynet closed her eyes and shook her head when she saw it. "That's not his room." Her fists clenched and she stood. She surveyed the room, biting her lip, then turned back to the table.

"Eldet, I've changed my mind," she said.

"About what?" he asked, straightening in his chair.

"You can use the rats to keep tracking her. They brought you here, and Kev's information seems to confirm it."

A grin broke out on Eldet's face and he slid his chair back as if to stand.

"I'm not done," Dynet said, holding up a hand. "You track her with the rats *if* you go with a pair of mage guards. I'll go ask these ones now." She tilted her head toward the two who had been talking to Mrs. Flowermiller. They now leaned against the cafe counter talking quietly to each other. Dynet approached the two women and spoke with them quietly for a moment, and then gestured towards the door. The mage guards nodded, smiled in Eldet's direction, then walked outside.

Dynet returned to their table. "Right. The tall, older one is Mage Netra, the younger one is Mage Purdale. You're to meet them outside. I've told them that the rats are Lyria's pets who have a special bond that allows them to find her, because I do *not* want the mage guard coming to us seeking a repeat performance for other cases, understand?" She looked down her nose sternly at Eldet, then with raised eyebrows at Kev as well.

Eldet nodded gravely.

Kev looked to her mother. "Can I follow with them?"

Her mother sighed. "I'd like to say no, but it seems you'll be in good hands with the mage guards, and they are your rats."

Ferra joined them too, and in moments the three friends were outside by the two mage guards, who greeted them with friendly smiles.

"Your mother said we're to escort you while you follow the girl's pet rats," said the one Dynet had identified as Mage Netra. She wore an amused but slightly puzzled expression as she said it.

"Yes, it's quite amazing," Eldet said, kneeling down beside the rucksack and beckoning the rats out of their hiding cubby. "They follow her everywhere, even when she tries to get them to stay home. That's how we thought of using them to find her."

"Good thinking," said Mage Purdale appreciatively.

Eldet grinned at Kev and handed Green Bean to her. She took the rat in her arms and waited while Eldet beckoned Turnip out of the pack. When he stood, he put Turnip in Kev's arms too, then bent down so he was face to face to the curious rodents. He gave each a morsel of the fish biscuit treats.

"Now, we thought we found her there, but she's gone. We have to find where she's been taken to." He held out a scrap of cloth for the rats to sniff. "This is the scent of the person who's taken her. And you know her scent, but here's her bracelet if you need it again. Now, do you think you can do that for us?"

The rats gave their answer by scrabbling down from Kev's arms by way of her tunic and leggings, then landing on the cobblestones of the square gracefully. They each ran in a different direction, but Eldet made no move to follow either one.

"They'll come back to us when they have the scent," he said at questioning looks from the mage guards.

Almost as soon as he said it, Green Bean came scurrying back from the back side of the Flowermiller Cafe and put her front paws up on Eldet's pant leg. Eldet gave her another tiny bit of the fish treat, and then Green Bean ran off again, this time stopping at the side of the building, waiting for them to follow.

They slipped between the Flowermiller Cafe and its neighboring building to arrive in the alley that Eldet, Kev, and Lyria had staked out several nights before. Turnip appeared from somewhere between the buildings and joined her sister in scurrying down the alley, hugging the sides of the buildings. Kev and her friends followed.

They left the alley at the next cross street and followed it to the left, slightly downhill in the direction of the lakeshore. The rats paused every now and then and seemed to sniff the air before moving on. Sometimes they would split up and go down different directions on cross streets before returning and confirming a direction by continuing that way together. The humans waited each time mostly in silence, Kev and her friends hoping the rats could find Lyria in time, the mage guards mostly seeming bemused at the rats.

They had gone several blocks farther toward the lakeshore district when the rats paused outside a brick two-story building. Eldet motioned for everyone to hold back, and they waited across the street while the rats approached the front door of the building. They stopped slightly to the side of the front door, then separated and both disappeared around the sides of the building.

Moments passed and Kev found herself clenching her fists.

"When can we go in?" Ferra asked beside her. She had been silent most of their walk here. Her voice wavered now.

"The rats have to tell us it's the right spot first," Eldet said.

"How will they do that?" asked Mage Purdale. Kev thought it was a good sign that she sounded more curious than skeptical.

They didn't need the mages deciding they couldn't follow the rats into the building.

Eldet scratched the back of his head. "Uh, well, I hadn't really thought that far. Usually they're finding little things that I hid that they can bring back to me."

"It sounds like you trained them for this," Mage Purdale said. "I thought your mother said we were following the rats because they belonged to the girl. Lyria."

"They do!" Eldet said in a rush. "It's just, we train them for fun too. Rats are smart."

"Indeed they are," came Mage Purdale's answer.

Before anyone could say anything more, Turnip came running as fast as her little rodent feet could carry her across the street to where they waited. She stopped at Eldet's feet and stood on her hind legs, resting her front paws on his pants again. He scooped her up. A moment later, Green Bean came running from the other side of the building. Both rats sat contentedly in Eldet's arms, making no moves to get down and start tracking again.

"I think this is it," Eldet said.

The mages nodded and the group approached the door to the building. It was locked, but Mage Netra put a finger to her lips and put a hand to the door, closing her eyes. She stood like that for mere seconds before opening her eyes again and turning the doorknob. The door swung open and the mages stepped inside.

"Wait here while we make sure it's safe," said Mage Netra.

"It's fine," came Mage Purdale's voice from ahead of Mage Netra.

Kev, Ferra, and Eldet followed the mages into the building. One of the mages called up a globe of mage light and illuminated the room they were in. It was a plain foyer with an empty desk at one end and several benches scattered throughout the room. It seemed to be an inn or a lodginghouse, with the front lobby closed for the night.

"Can they show us which room?" Mage Purdale asked. "If we

can get in and out without disturbing the other tenants, we'll be lucky indeed."

At Eldet's word, the rats jumped from his outstretched hands onto the lobby floor. They went directly to the stairway on the right, then paused at the bottom step and looked back.

"I guess that's it," Ferra said, looking to the two mages.

"Wait here," said Mage Netra to Kev and her friends.

The mages turned and followed the rats up the stairs.

DISCOVERY

Kev watched wordlessly as the two mages disappeared up the stairs. Though she understood why it had to be the mages who went first, she itched to be the one following the rats right now. Lyria was hurt, and she needed to help her. She needed to do something.

She looked to Eldet and Ferra, who stood near the bottom of the stairs with her. They both shared her feelings too, judging by their expressions. Eldet opened his mouth as if to say something, but before he could, shouting sounded above them.

A person appeared at the top of the stairs, running at full speed, the pounding of his feet reverberating through the quiet building. He descended the stairs two at a time, barreling straight toward Kev and her friends.

"Get out of the way!" he shouted, or at least it sounded close to that; his words seemed to blur together.

Instinctively, Kev had moved away when she saw him running down the stairs, as had Eldet and Ferra. But at the last second, as he came to the bottom steps and closer to the freedom of the front door beyond, Kev's brain caught up to what was happening, and she recognized him. It was Dinnan. And he was running from the mages.

She stuck her foot out. Dinnan tripped and landed on his face on the lobby floor.

"Don't let him up!" shouted Mage Purdale from the stairs above. She ran fast too, but not as frantically as Dinnan had, so it took her longer to come down the stairs.

Kev did the only thing she could think of and threw herself onto Dinnan. Ferra did the same, while Eldet closed his eyes and held his hands out in Dinnan's direction, doing some kind of magic that Kev couldn't see.

Dinnan's shouting hadn't stopped. He gabbled into the floor where he was pinned.

"I didn't mean to do it! I didn't mean to hurt her. I just wanted to see the magic, that's all I wanted. I just wanted to see how it worked," he said, repeating the sentences over and over as he struggled against Kev's grip. "I'm sorry, I really didn't mean to do it. I was trying to get help, I was. He said he could help her but he made it worse! I didn't mean to, I swear."

"You can let go," said Mage Purdale when she reached them. With a gesture of Mage Purdale's hand, Kev felt Dinnan's struggling lessen, then cease. His shouting and sobbing grew more garbled, then slowed, then stopped.

Kev and Ferra stood and backed away from Dinnan's no longer struggling form. Now that Kev could see his face, she saw that he had fallen asleep.

"Where's Lyria?" Ferra asked, standing and panting.

"First floor," Mage Purdale said, nodding towards the stairs. "Netra is with her. I've already sent for help."

Ferra took off up the stairs at a run.

Kev backed away from Dinnan and glanced between his prone form and the stairs. She saw Eldet hesitating too.

"You can go up," Mage Purdale said, understanding their hesitation. "He won't wake any time soon. I'll send the riders up when they get here."

"Thank you," Kev and Eldet said in unison, and then ran up the stairs after Ferra.

The room was exactly as Kev had drawn it. It was small and sparse, with a bed in one corner, a desk across from it, and the sofa that Lyria was slumped over at the opposite end of the room. A small rug in front of the door separated the two halves of the room. Another person who Kev didn't recognize lay on the bed, apparently sleeping, but Kev assumed the mages had subdued him the same way they had Dinnan. Either that, or he was another of Dinnan's victims.

Mage Netra stood over Lyria behind the couch, keeping her gaze fixed on the girl. Ferra knelt on the floor before her, holding one of her hands and watching her face. The rats had crawled up onto the couch and wriggled their way onto Lyria's lap, snuggling into the folds of her skirt.

"She's alive, but unconscious," said Mage Netra. "I can't try to reverse it until I find out exactly what he did that caused this. We'll need to bring her to the healer's hall at the Outpost."

"Is it safe to move her?" Kev asked. The Outpost was fairly far up the hill from this building.

"The dragons can transport her safely," said Mage Netra, nodding in understanding at Kev's concern.

Ferra suddenly shivered and sat up, jolted out of her watchfulness. "We'll need to tell her parents," she said. She started to rise from the floor. "I need to go to the wagons."

"Sit," said Mage Netra. "We've sent messages to the mages at the Outpost, and they'll make sure the news gets where it needs to go."

Ferra nodded and relaxed again. "What can I do?" she said quietly.

Mage Netra put a hand on Ferra's shoulder. "You're doing everything you can. Staying with her is enough. It'll ground her."

It wasn't long before they heard voices outside and footsteps on the stairs. A few of the occupants of the other rooms in the building poked their heads out to watch as dragon riders and mage guards clomped up the stairs and into the room where Lyria lay waiting.

Carefully, two of the mage guards used their magic to lift Lyria from the sofa and float her sleeping form down the stairs to where a dragon waited with a soft, padded platform strapped to its back. They lay Lyria atop the platform and strapped her to it, then lay blankets atop her. One of the mages joined the dragon rider on the dragon's back, perched behind Lyria, while the rider rode in front of it near the dragon's neck.

Now that more dragon riders and the mage guard had arrived, the mages allowed Dinnan and the other man to awaken from their magic-induced slumber. Dinnan almost immediately returned to his incoherent blubbering, but at a pointedly raised eyebrow from Mage Purdale, he quieted down again.

Kev's mother had arrived on dragonback with Eldet's mother. As the mage guard and dragon riders took care of everything, Kev and her friends stood with her mother and Dynet within the warm embrace of Riki's tail. The rats had returned to Kev when the mage guard were readying Lyria to be moved, and Kev now had her rucksack with the secret rat compartment back. Kev clutched the pack in front of her and leaned back on Riki's side, enjoying the warmth that emanated from the dragon's scales. Her eyes drooped, and then she found herself startling awake when her head dipped backwards, bumping Riki's side.

Her mother put an arm around her. "It's time to go home," she said. "There's nothing more we can do to help tonight."

Kev nodded and stifled a yawn.

"I'll bring you both," said Dynet, standing near Riki's head and gesturing towards the saddle on the dragon's back.

Ferra and Eldet waved from where they were perched on another dragon's back, then Kev mounted Riki after her mother. She managed to stay awake for the short ride back to her home, then stumbled to her bed and fell immediately to sleep.

HEALER'S HALL

Three days later, Lyria was finally allowed to have visitors in her room at the Outpost healer's hall. During the three days that they waited to see her, Kev learned from Eldet that it had taken two full days for the healer mages to break the spell that Dinnan had cast on her. It had only been so difficult because Dinnan couldn't adequately explain what he had done. Through many rounds of interviews, the mage guard learned that Dinnan had done whatever it was that caused her to black out while she was in his rooms above the Flowermiller Cafe. Then, when he'd been unsuccessful in waking her, he had brought her to the other mage in the lodginghouse where they'd been found that night.

Dinnan was still being held for a hearing by the judge, and the other mage had been allowed to go after he'd told his story—he'd barely been involved, and he had only been trying to help Lyria at Dinnan's request.

Kev arrived at the Outpost on foot, carrying her rucksack with the rats firmly ensconced in their hidden sleeping pouch. After the gate guard let her through, she walked through the gate and down the path into the yard, then looked about. Across the grassy field of the yard, she saw Eldet's figure bounce up from where he had been lying under a tree. He waved to Kev and ran over. Together, they walked to the wing of the Outpost building that held the healer's hall, where mages with corresponding abilities worked as healers.

Kev had never been here before; nobody in her family had needed a mage healer for anything, fortunately. They'd always had a non-mage doctor come to their house for minor ailments. She followed Eldet into the building on the ground floor, sparing a glance for the dragon that perched on the corner of the building above, sunning itself in the bright morning light.

Just inside the doors there was a desk where two women sat chatting, and beyond the desk there was yet another set of doors. The women quieted when Kev and Eldet entered the first doors and smiled.

"Hello Eldet," said one of the women. "Here to see Lyria?"

"Yes, and I have my friend Keveren Auberel to visit as well," he answered.

The woman smiled and pushed a logbook across the desk toward them. "Just sign in here, and then we'll take you to her room."

They did as instructed, and when they were finished, the second woman rose from her seat and led them through the next set of doors. The room beyond was fairly large, with several groupings of furniture spread about. It must be a waiting room, Kev thought. To the left, there was a sign for the infirmary, and to the right a door with a sign that simply said "Rooms." The woman led them to the door with the "rooms" sign and they entered a little hall. At the second door down the hallway, the woman paused and knocked.

"Come in," came the faint response.

The woman opened the door and gestured for Kev and Eldet to enter, then left them with Lyria.

Lyria sat propped against a stack of pillows, a book open on her lap. She smiled when she saw Kev and Eldet enter. She looked tired, with circles under her eyes and a halfhearted smile.

"I heard you rescued me," she said. Her voice was softer than usual, and a little scratchy, as if she had lost it from screaming or shouting too much. Perhaps she had.

"Rescued?" Eldet said, scratching his head. "Nah, the mage guard and the dragon riders did the rescuing part," he said.

"They said they only found me because of you. You and the rats," she said, looking at Eldet. She turned to Kev. "And you. Your drawings. Does that mean you finally got your sketch magic working?"

"Uh, it turns out it was working all along," Kev said ruefully. "I just wasn't listening to it right." Then her stomach dipped when she remembered that her faulty information might have gotten Lyria into trouble in the first place. "I'm sorry if what I told you about my sketches caused any of this," she said. "I'm so sorry."

"Don't you dare," said Lyria, still softly, but fiercely too. "I was stupid," she said, shaking her head. "I shouldn't have gone to Dinnan's in the first place."

"Um, what exactly did happen?" Eldet said. "My ma hasn't told me much. From your side, that is. We have some of Dinnan's story, but how did you end up in his lodging room?"

Lyria closed her eyes and shook her head. "I never should have gone to Dinnan's, but I did." She looked to Kev before saying the next part. "And yes, I did go to him because of what you told me about Yeran and Tanar. But," she said, holding her hand up, palm facing Kev, "I was already thinking of going there anyway. He had been talking to me in the art library, actually, after we asked him about my jewelry case the first time. And he actually seemed really nice for a bit there. He said he was so interested in all of the art that students at the Scholar's Tower made, and that he wished he could do it to, but he didn't have that kind of talent." She shook her head again. "And that was sort of true, but he meant craft-magic. He could *see* craftmagic."

"What do you mean?" Kev asked, a shiver going through her.

"I never knew he was a mage, but he is. And when I got to his rooms, he was all excited, and he asked me to make something while he watched. He—he had my jewelry case with all my supplies that were missing," she said angrily. "I almost left, but the way he explained himself, it made me feel sorry for him." She paused and glowered at her lap. "He's a mage, and he wanted to study craftmagic, because he can see it in his mage sight, just like regular magic."

Eldet frowned in confusion. He had been sitting there, looking like he wanted to say something, for the last few minutes. "But they're different kinds of magic! That shouldn't be possible!"

"Most mages don't even believe craftmagic exists," Kev said.

"That's right," Lyria said with a nod. "Dinnan said that was why he couldn't study it. Other mages that he told about it couldn't see it, so they didn't think it was real. They told him he was just seeing the craftsperson's normal energy, like what mages usually can see."

Lyria sighed and glowered at her lap for a moment before continuing on.

"So I did a bracelet while he watched with his mage sight," she said. "I figured, if I did what he asked, then he would let me go, and I could get my supplies case back. He *said* he only wanted to *watch* me work. With his mage sight. But he did something else. It must have been the same thing he did on the day he stole my case, when the bead I picked up was so hot. It was like, I don't know, like he was trying to take the magic for his own. I felt his magic join mine, or—or something. I don't really know how to explain it. But then I started to feel really warm, and I kept getting hotter and hotter, and I tried to stop working, and then Dinnan was yelling at me to keep going, that he almost had it. I don't know what he meant. But I couldn't keep going. I was sweating so much. And then I must have just passed out. And then I woke up here."

"Was he trying to *steal* your craftmagic?" Eldet said, looking baffled and disgusted at the same time.

"I think so," Lyria whispered. She took a shaky breath, then continued. "I told the mage guards who came to talk to me everything he said. I couldn't tell what they thought. I didn't exactly admit to actually having craftmagic. I more just repeated everything Dinnan said. So if they don't believe in it, they'll just think he's a loon."

"He's a loon anyway," Eldet muttered.

Kev had been watching Lyria thoughtfully as she told her story, and thinking about her own craftmagic. She had doubted it, been unsure of herself when using it, and her doubt had led her astray. But craftmagic was real, Dinnan was proof. If mages could see it, even only some of them, then it had to be real.

That didn't help her get any farther with trying to understand just exactly what it could do and how to use it, but the alleviation of her doubts helped her see a path forward. She couldn't rely on knowledge compiled by mages who didn't believe in craftmagic to learn about it. She would have to discover her abilities for herself. Possibly with help from her friends.

"Did you say you got your crafting case back?" Kev asked.

Lyria's face lit up. "Yes! The mage guard wanted to examine it first, since Dinnan was talking about me using it for magic, but the guards said they didn't see anything but jewelry, and gave it back. I got almost all of my finished pieces back, too. I think Dinnan may have burned some, trying to examine them." Her frown returned at that last statement.

"So you can finish out the last week of the fair!" Kev said.

Lyria's smile returned. "Yes, if I feel well enough."

"You will," Kev said, hoping it was true. No, she believed it was true. Lyria would finish the fair, and Kev would help her if she needed it.

Turnip and Green Bean must have had enough of their nap in their cozy carrier by now, for they suddenly emerged from the hidden opening, poking their heads out just far enough to sniff the air and look around the room.

Lyria laughed and put a hand to her mouth. "What's this?"

she asked, giggling at the sight of the rats' heads and nothing else. The rats then squirmed out and crawled into Lyria's lap, settling in to be petted. "They allowed you two in here?"

"I've sort of given up on trying to keep them from following me everywhere," Kev said. "At Master Rithorn's advice. He's the master of Eldet's apprenticeship in creature magic."

"He's the one who gave me a lot of the training ideas for teaching the rats to track things," Eldet said. "And that's how they found you."

"You're such good little rats, aren't you?" Lyria crooned down at the two creatures in her lap. They ground their teeth and boggled their eyes at the praise lavished on them as Lyria stroked from between their ears down their backs. "Of course you deserve to go everywhere Kev goes."

"It hardly seems like I have a choice," Kev said, sighing. "But I do have to say, it's been a lot easier going along with it than it was trying to keep the rats at home. And who knows? Maybe their tracking abilities will come in handy again one day."

"I know they will," Lyria said.

Return to the Scholar's Tower

Kev returned to school the next week after taking the rest of the week off following Lyria's kidnapping and, now seemingly more distant, Tanar's assault on her. News of both incidents had reached the school, Ferra had told her, and Kev thought she noticed a few surreptitious glances her way as she walked to her first class. There was nothing she could do about it, though, so she squared her shoulders and stood tall as she made her way to History of Magic.

Mage Valaso gave her a brief nod as she entered his classroom, but didn't say anything as she found a seat and prepared for the lecture. She set her new rucksack down at her feet, sending a silent thought to the rats that they must stay inside their hiding pouch while they were inside the Scholar's Tower. Of course they couldn't read her mind, but the repetition of the rules comforted her just the same. She'd said the same thing aloud to the rats enough times before she allowed them into the rucksack that she knew they understood the rules *and* the consequences of breaking them. If they got her in trouble in school, she would go back to Master Rithorn and find out a way to keep them home for good.

There was no sign of Tanar or Yeran in History of Magic class that day, nor would there be on any other day. In the days following Lyria's rescue from Dinnan, Kev's mother had insisted on immediate meetings with those in charge at the Scholar's Tower instead of waiting for a hearing. She had made Kev attend one of the meetings to tell her own side of the story. Kev had given her honest accounting of the events before a truthsaying mage, who had the ability to tell if a person was lying or otherwise twisting their words. The school official in charge of hearing Kev's statement assured her that Tanar and Yeran would be doing the same in their own meetings.

Not more than a day later, Kev's mother got a message from the Scholar's Tower informing her that Kev could continue to attend all of her classes as normal, and that Tanar and Yeran would no longer be allowed on the premises of the Scholar's Tower. Kev breathed a sigh of relief to hear that, but part of her wondered where Tanar and Yeran would go now. She hoped she never ran into them in the city again. She probably wouldn't, since she didn't run in the same circles as merchant's children did, anyway.

When the class was over, Mage Valaso called Kev up to talk to him as he had the other day when he'd warned her of Tanar's claims against her.

"I'm sorry," he said immediately when she reached the front of the classroom. "I didn't mean to enable the kind of behavior that Tanar was engaging in toward you. I wasn't aware of the whole situation. It won't happen again."

"Thank you," said Kev. Not knowing what else to say, she gave him what she hoped was an appreciative-looking smile, and turned to leave.

"One more thing," Mage Valaso said.

Kev stopped.

"I've heard some rumors that you have some remarkable pet rats," he said. There was a slight twinkle in his eye. "Mage raised? And that they helped track a missing student?"

Kev nodded slowly. Did he know that she had them in her

pack? Would she get in trouble for having them at the Scholar's Tower?

But Mage Valaso was grinning. "I used to have some pet rats myself. Not mage raised, of course." Then he looked wistful. "But perhaps if they had been, they would have lived longer. The short life span of rodents is such a shame."

"It is," Kev agreed. "We don't know if mine will live longer, though. My friend who's an apprentice mage thinks they will."

"I hope so," Mage Valaso said with a smile. "Well, if it's not too much trouble, I would like to meet yours sometime."

Kev laughed in surprise and unshouldered her rucksack. She tapped on the outside of the compartment where Green Bean and Turnip had obediently stayed throughout the whole class.

"Would you like to come out for a bit?" she asked.

Mage Valaso gave a disbelieving chuckle as the two rats squirmed out of their hidden compartment and into Kev's arms.

"I certainly wasn't expecting that," he said. "What a clever pack."

"I tried to get them to stay in their cage at home, but it wasn't working," Kev said, warming up to the subject. "They're too smart for their own good."

"I'll say," Mage Valaso said, holding a hand out for the rats to sniff. Green Bean put her paws on Mage Valaso's fingers and took an exploratory nibble.

"Green Bean!" Kev said, shocked.

Mage Valaso laughed a hearty laugh. "Mage raised or not, I suppose they're still rats. May I give them a treat?"

At Kev's assent, Mage Valaso dug in his bag and produced a somewhat crumpled pastry. He broke off two pieces and gave them to the rats.

"Oh, I do miss my rats," he said. "Maybe I'll have to get some of my own again."

The bell began to chime for the next hour's class, and Kev hurriedly coaxed the rats back into their hidden pouch.

"I won't breathe a word," Mage Valaso said with a smile, then took a bite from his pastry. "Again, I'm sorry for what happened with Tanar," he said one last time before packing up his books and heading out the door.

By the end of the week, everything had, for the most part, settled into a new normal. Kev and Ferra brought Lyria notes and reading assignments from her classes for a couple of days until Lyria was ready to leave her room at the healer's hall. Once she was recovered, Lyria began attending her classes again and then going directly to the Onami fair to sell her jewelry, which was well received. She displayed some pieces in her parents' stall outside their wagon, and wandered the fair with a portable display board full of bracelets, necklaces, and even some larger adornments, like beaded belts and ties to wind in one's hair. Kev and Ferra joined her as often as they could during that final week of the fair.

Now that the thieves had been caught and the artisans' goods and supplies had been returned, the atmosphere at the fair felt especially light and joyful. Lyria said that her parents reported that many of the Onami families who had been packed and ready to flee now breathed easier. They could enjoy the fair fully now that the thieves had been caught.

Kev did wonder about one thing. "My uncle said that before his things were stolen, his mortar and pestle were hot. Like your bead was before Dinnan stole it," Kev said. "But now we know Dinnan didn't steal any of the things at the fair. So why were my uncle's things warm like when Dinnan looked at your craftmagic?"

Lyria and Ferra stopped in their tracks. Lyria frowned at Kev, clearly perturbed. "I don't know. Nobody mentioned that part once the thieves were caught. They were just a bunch of people trying to resell stuff at the docks, right?"

"That's what Eldet's ma said," Ferra said.

"It's what the mage guard told everyone in the Onami caravan, too," Lyria said. "My parents said they assured them the thefts were not meant to target the Onami specifically. They just wanted valuable items to resell."

"You told me before that the only Onami craftspeople who'd been stolen from used craftmagic, right?" Kev asked.

"Yes," said Lyria, "but it must have been a coincidence. It had to have been."

"Or the mage guard ignored it," Ferra said. "Like they ignored Dinnan's rantings and ravings about your craftmagic." She looked pointedly at Lyria. "They don't believe in it, so they don't see it."

Kev sucked in a breath. Ferra was right.

"So Dinnan's not the only mage who can see the workings of craftmagic," Kev said slowly. "The market thieves were looking for it too. They just used it to find out what to steal, not to try to suck the magic out of the craft mages like Dinnan did."

"Should I tell my parents?" Lyria said, biting her lip. "Everybody was so happy to learn that the Onami with craftmagic weren't being targeted."

"You can tell them," Ferra said. "So they know that there are some mages out there who know how to look for it. But I don't think they need to worry about the mage guard or anyone coming after you for bound magic."

Lyria sucked in a breath and blew it out. "You're right," she said. Then she shook herself, smiled, and turned toward the stream of people meandering through the fair. She held her jewelry display board high and strode confidently onward.

Kev watched her friend with a smile and pondered their conversation. Maybe she hadn't been able to find more books about craftmagic, but maybe she didn't need to.

Kev's mother was still visiting the fair each day too, whether she was selling yarn and dyestuffs at Aunt Kalla and Uncle Vansal's stall or making her way around to other stalls trading for supplies that she'd use in her spinning and dyeing during the coming year. Kev returned home with her mother each night sore and bone-weary, but content.

Despite her weariness and her full days, Kev made time every night to do a sketch of some kind, no matter how small. She had purchased a new journal full of sketch paper at the Onami fair, nothing fancy, just a book of paper bound with paper board and tied closed with a red string. Often she gravitated towards fancier notebooks and journals, but for this, she needed to feel as if she could just sketch in it without worrying that she should to save it for something more important. She needed to let the sketches just be what they were, without trying too hard. She needed to practice.

That was the conclusion Kev had come to regarding her sketch magic. Without a master to train her, like Eldet in his apprenticeship with Master Rithorn, and without books and records to learn from, all Kev had left was herself. She would have to learn about and improve her abilities one step at a time, and trust herself. Of course, she would still keep her eyes and ears open for any new resources that could help her learn more about what she had, but she didn't need to know it all now. Learning was a process, and she would spend the rest of her life developing her skill.

One of these days, though, she was going to ask her ma about her spinning and dyeing. If she was right, her mother had some craftmagic herself, and while it wasn't sketching, Kev was sure she could learn something from her. She yawned, then smiled as she sketched. She would make her own apprenticeships.

Last Day at the Fair

On the very last day of the Onami Fair, the tradition was for the dragon riders to do a flying show in combination with a light show put on by mages from the Mage Academy. Kev and her entire family attended the fair together on this day, and it was her mother's chance to attend the fair without selling or buying or otherwise having to conduct business.

Business in many of the goods and craft stalls tapered off as well, but the last day of the fair was one of the biggest days for food and drink sellers. That was because, in addition to the dragon and light show in the evening, there were many additional performances of all kinds throughout the day, all around the fair grounds. Musicians, play actors, acrobats, jugglers, storytellers, and performers of all kinds and skill levels could come to the fair and display their talents on the final day. Some got places at the stages and raised platforms throughout the fairgrounds, others wandered in and out of the crowds near the foodsellers' stalls.

Though Kev was normally a quiet person and preferred less energetic activities, she could appreciate the atmosphere of the Onami fair on its last day once per year. The sun had granted them another glowing autumn day, and although she carried her rucksack with her, the rats chose to ride perched on her shoulders as she wandered the fair with her enthusiastic siblings. To her surprise, nobody seemed to care about the rats beyond a few puzzled stares. Maybe her fear of them being noticed was overblown. And exacerbated by Tanar's bullying, she thought. But now, in the warm, welcoming embrace of her people's song, food, and dance, she felt right at home, even with her unusual pets partaking in the festivities as well.

As the sun began to settle in the warm autumn evening, torches were lit outside of stalls and bordering the pathways and stages throughout the fairgrounds. Kev and her family had found themselves an open patch of grass on a slope in the field that bordered the fairgrounds, where many people gathered to watch the sky show. They spread out thick woolen blankets to sit on and took turns running off to food sellers to get their favorite foods. Kev's father returned to the blanket with his thermos full of hot apple cider, which he divided out into small wooden cups he'd brought for all of them.

Green Bean and Turnip slid down from Kev's shoulders into her lap and cuddled into the hole made by her crisscrossed legs. From there, they accepted offerings of treats from Kev and Sayess, who giggled every time their whiskers tickled her fingers. When the sun sank even lower in the sky and Kev's legs began to chill, she threw a shawl from her rucksack over her lap, and the rats settled in for a rest.

A bugling sound cut through the chill air and the crowd hushed. Against the deepening blue of the sky, the silhouette of a dragon launched into view. It called out again, and another shape joined it. They circled each other in the air, then blew twin blasts of flame up into the night sky. They called again and more dragons joined them until there were at least a dozen dragons; Kev lost count. They danced and swirled against the sky, sending out flames in different patterns, or swooping out over the fairgrounds and then returning to their places against the steadily darkening starry canvas.

Kev remembered how she had used to shiver under the dance

of the dragons, how the thought of them had made her squirm before she'd gotten to know some riders, and by extension their dragons. Now she could enjoy the performance as much as her family always had. She wondered if one of them was Riki, and if Eldet's ma Dynet was up there flying around. She smiled.

When the sky had gone completely dark, the mage lights started. The dragons had become almost invisible against the dark night sky, except as patches of darkness against the light of the stars. Then the sky burst into layers of undulating light, and the dragons could be seen again. The dragons themselves were illuminated, somehow outlined by lines of mage light in different colors, tracing the shape of their heads, their necks, their wings as they flew through the night sky.

The next time the dragons flew out over the crowds, showers of light fell from them like scattered embers from a fire. The people in the crowd gasped and reached up to touch the falling sparks of light, but the lights faded as they sank to the earth.

Next, two dragons rose up in mock battle, their glowing figures acting out a fight like the ancient dragons had once done before they had bonded with humans, before Arethia had been born. At the end of the mock battle, the two lighted figures clashed and then appeared to fall from the sky, disappearing as the lights on them winked out.

After that, the mages took over the light show, and music swelled up around them, played by a group near the back of the field, but amplified by magic so that everyone could hear it. Kev basked in the glow of the mage lights dancing in pictures through the sky, letting herself take in the display that at some times showed figures and stories, while others simply flashed and danced in abstract shapes.

"I want to be a dragon rider someday," Sayess whispered at Kev's side.

Kev smiled and bumped her shoulder gently against Sayess's. "I'll go with you when you go to a hatching," she said to her little sister.

In the glow from the mage lights, Kev could see Sayess grinning up at her.

"What do you want to be, Kev?"

"I want to be a scholar, you know that. Someone who always keeps learning."

"No, I mean after that," Sayess said.

Kev opened her mouth, ready to launch into an explanation for her sister that even after she completed all her years as a student at the Scholar's Tower, she would still be a scholar, but then she closed it and thought a bit longer. She'd always pictured herself studying forever, probably becoming one of the professors who taught at the Scholar's Tower. But she could imagine other things, too. So she told her sister one of those.

"I'd like to be an artist," she said. "And when you get your dragon and become a rider, I'll paint a portrait of you with your dragon. How about that?"

Sayess giggled and lay her head against Kev's arm. Kev wrapped her arm around her little sister's shoulders.

By the end of the sky show, the night had grown cooler, and the food and drink sellers, performers, and caravan vendors had all begun to pack up their things. In the morning, the Onami caravan would begin its slow roll down the road to the shore of Lake Morna and then continue on its route around the western edge of the lake, before it would turn south towards the plains, then Areth.

Kev and her family packed up their blanket and all of the trinkets they'd got at the fair, and stopped by Kalla and Vansal's stall to say one last goodbye. They wouldn't see them again until the caravan headed back northward in the spring.

Once at home, Kev flopped onto her bed after saying goodnight to her family and helping to tuck Sayess into bed. The rats had snuck under the covers with Sayess, much to Sayess's delight and Kev's chagrin. Once in her own bed, Kev resisted the urge to close her eyes and took out her sketchbook instead. She was determined not to miss a night of her sketching.

As she sketched, she thought back over the last couple weeks. School had barely started for the year, and she already felt like it had been ages since her first day at the Scholar's Tower. So much had happened, and she'd already missed more classes than she'd ever thought would be allowed. Next week, she would get serious about catching up on her studies and get into a good routine. She smiled at the sketch that formed on the paper before her. A desk, a book, and a cup of pencils. Yes, now that the fair was over, and Lyria's jewelry supply case had been found, she could focus on her studies. Kev put her sketchbook away and snuggled down under her blanket. She looked forward to the coming weeks of nice, quiet routine.

As she dozed off, thinking about how a visit to her favorite library cafe in the dockmarket district was in store, she felt the rats nudge their way under her blankets and snuggle close to her.

Yep. The rest of the year would be full of quiet studying and warm, familiar routine.

"Isn't that right, rats?" she whispered.

The rats snuggled against her arm and ground their teeth in contentment.

"That's right," Kev said for them, and drifted off to sleep.

ABOUT THE AUTHOR

Nikki Bollman is the author of the Dragons of Arethia trilogy and other fantasy fiction. When she's not writing, she can be found knitting and spinning yarn, hiking with her family and adorable but moody rescue husky, or reading in her hammock.

Also by Nikki Bollman

Thank you for reading The Weyrdragon and the Fire Agate Necklace! I hope you enjoyed this first book in the Keveren Auberel Mysteries series. Visit my website at SticksandScribbles.com and join my email list to get updated when a new book is added to the series, and you'll get a bonus short story!

Keveren Auberel Mysteries

The Weyrdragon and the Fire Agate Necklace

Stolen Magic at the Onami Fair

Dragons of Arethia Trilogy

Tesa's Journey

Binding Magic

Fate of Dragons

Short Story Collection

Fairy Stories

Visit My Website

SticksandScribbles.com

Ingram Content Group UK Ltd.
Milton Keynes UK
UKHW020915190723
425423UK00001B/79